HANG TIME

A GENUINE RARE BIRD BOOK
LOS ANGELES, CALIF.

A GREG SALEM MYSTERY

HANG TIME

S. W. LAUDEN

THIS IS A GENUINE RARE BIRD BOOK

A Rare Bird Book | Rare Bird Books
453 South Spring Street, Suite 302
Los Angeles, CA 90013
rarebirdbooks.com

FIRST TRADE PAPERBACK ORIGINAL EDITION

This is a work of fiction, all of the characters and events in this story are imagined.

Set in Minion Pro
Printed in the United States

Book Design by Robert Schlofferman

10 9 8 7 6 5 4 3 2 1

Publisher's Cataloging-in-Publication data
Names: Lauden, S. W., author.
Title: Hang time : a Greg Salem mystery / S. W. Lauden
Series: Greg Salem Mystery
Description: First Trade Paperback Original Edition | A Genuine Rare Bird
Book | New York, NY; Los Angeles, CA: Rare Bird Books, 2018.
Identifiers: ISBN 9781945572715
Subjects: LCSH Musicians—Fiction. | Rock music—Fiction. | Los Angeles
(Calif.)—Fiction. | Mystery and detective stories. | Suspense fiction. | BISAC
FICTION / Mystery & Detective / General.
Classification: LCC PS3612.A9323 G75 2018 | DDC 813.6—dc23

Also by S. W. Lauden

Bad Citizen Corporation
Grizzly Season
Crosswise
Crossed Bones

October 1998—11:00 p.m.

Tim threw the rope over the exposed ceiling beam. He'd been practicing the move in his mind all day, but it still took a few tries. A sense of relief washed over him as he looped it over again, pulling the loose end down the other side to form a noose. His mind was surprisingly sharp considering the farewell shot of heroin coursing through his veins.

He'd learned about tying knots from his father, at their cabin in the mountains. The family spent whole summers up there when he and his younger brother, Greg, were still kids. Just three men hunting, fishing, and living off the land. Tears filled his eyes as he thought about how much simpler life had been then. Before they discovered punk rock, drugs, and disappointment in their teenage years. Tim wondered if his father or brother would recognize the knot when they found his body.

Tim took a step back to have a last look around the record store. A familiar yellow glow came through the windows from the streetlights out front. The towering racks and bursting bins always looked like an industrial landscape to him, silhouetted as they were in the crowded space. Only he knew exactly where every rare single and limited edition remastered CD was tucked away. This was the business he'd built with his own two hands, dropping out of high school to devote himself to music.

He'd worked endless hours every day since, toiling alone in the tiny backroom office—teaching himself how to read foreign catalogs, understand basic accounting, and occasionally make payroll. It was a labor of love that reaped its meager rewards in the frantic smiles of his devoted teenage customers; the same kids who used to come see his band, Bad Citizen Corporation, play at the local all-ages venues.

That was before the band he loved ruined his life. There had been plenty of evidence that things were changing. It was there in pointless power struggles at the rehearsal studio, where he and Greg fought over things as trivial as set lists. Or in the tour van when they'd come to blows over which fast-food restaurant to drive through, or which song to listen to on the stereo.

And it was there at their childhood home where they could no longer visit their father at the same time. Tim could see how it hurt the old man, but there was nothing he or anybody else could do about it. He understood now how he'd retreated into ritualistic self-destruction that required something as blunt as a needle for relief. He'd chosen to shut himself down instead of facing the pain of his band—his *life*— falling apart. Greg, on the other hand, embraced anger; clutching tight to his ego as he waded fists-first into fight after pointless fight. There simply wasn't enough oxygen to contain them together in their father's house, the band, or, as Tim very recently realized, the entire world.

Tim saw it all much more clearly now, framed through the noose swinging in front of his face. The finality of it all brought a sort of clarity to his mind, a sad certainty that every one of those signs lined the one-way street leading him here. There was a terrible inevitability to it, a tired junkie cliché that almost made him laugh.

He climbed up onto the counter, slipping the noose around his neck. The rope felt itchy against his skin, a brief reminder of the petty annoyances he was saying goodbye to forever. He slid the knot down until it was tight, inching his Converse to the edge. It was no longer a question of *if*, but *when*.

Tim barely finished whispering "Goodbye" before leaping out into the permanent darkness. He listened to the rope creak against the ceiling beam overhead, mind already disconnected from his arched back and jerking legs. It came as a shock when, in his final moments, he still had more questions than answers. One in particular was louder than all the rest—*Will Greg ever understand why I had to do this for him?*

Chapter 1

Greg Salem shattered the backstage mirror with his clenched fist. Tiny shards of blood-splattered glass rained down on his Converse and danced across the sticky concrete floor. Satisfying jolts of pain shot up his arm as he lowered the mangled hand to his side. A hundred little reflections judged him now, the mocking eyes of a spider in a jagged web of destruction.

He hated everything about the fraud staring back at him, starting with his ridiculous burgundy hair. His best friend Junior did the dye job earlier that day in an effort to cover up the rogue greys. There was nothing she could do about the tiny lines clinging to his eyes like claw marks, or the longer ones etched into his forehead. They were almost more noticeable these days than the slowly fading tattoos poking up from under the collar of his Black Flag T-shirt.

Greg should have been walking on air, but his self-doubt had an undeniable gravity. He couldn't imagine why anybody would pay to watch a forty-one-year-old man up on stage, even though the show had sold out in minutes. And now here they were, crammed into Eddie's L Bar to see the first stop of Bad Citizen Corporation's official reunion.

His stomach was all knots as he listened to the crowd through the flimsy door. They got louder as they sucked down drinks, screaming to be heard over the barrage of old-school hardcore blaring from the speakers. Junior's son, Chris, created the playlist; selecting favorites from the steady diet of bands Greg fed him in preparation for their upcoming tour. At thirteen Chris was the youngest member of the band by almost three decades, and the only one of them that couldn't legally be in the club.

Greg's gaze drifted to the busted mirror. He listened as 98 Mute's "Another Boring Day" gave way to "Richard Hung Himself" by D.I. The walls of the tiny storage closet dressing room were covered in fading memories of the countless bands that had played there over the years. Layers of cracked and peeling stickers were interwoven with intricate, hand-drawn logos making the space feel even more suffocating than it already was. There was barely enough room for a couple of chairs and a few guitar cases. The air choked with the smell of stale beer and dank sweat.

The rest of the band was out wandering the crowd, giving Greg his space. These days the lineup included the original rhythm section of JJ on bass and Marco on drums, along with a new guitarist named Jerry that their label suggested to balance out Chris. Everybody at Dead March Records loved the idea of a thirteen-year-old guitarist for publicity, but not so much when show time rolled around.

Greg paced in circles, stalking his thoughts. He had some serious doubts about this BCC reunion. The money was pretty good and definitely helped him sleep a little easier with a family to support, but playing music had never felt like such a job. He barely saw Kristen any more between the private investigation work he picked up and the band's sporadic practices. And when he was home, she'd shove their son into his arms before sneaking off for a shower or nap. The days of coming home to find her sunbathing topless in the backyard were gone, and so were their long nights between the sheets. She'd become a different woman now; a person Greg feared he'd never truly know.

He dropped down into a rickety chair, his knee pumping nervously as he wiped blood from his hand with a damp bar towel. Playing music was better than bartending—*or being a cop for that matter*—but it didn't calm his nerves. "Lights Out" by Angry Samoans came on and Greg thought he heard a fight start somewhere inside of Eddie's. A burst of adrenaline flooded his veins; he leapt up and singed his hair on an exposed light bulb dangling low from the rafters overhead. It swayed back and forth, throwing the small space into a riot of shadow and light.

Greg reached for one of the electric guitars leaning against the wall, giving it a vicious strum. Two strings snapped as the pick sawed downward with all the grace of a steak knife through a beer can. He dropped the instrument to the ground and went back over to the mirror. Only a few minutes left before they hit the stage, but Greg was ready to crawl out of his skin. He needed something to take the edge off. *I worked at this bar for almost a year and I never craved a drink this bad.*

Falling off the wagon wasn't an option. Not *ever*, but especially not tonight in front of his hometown crowd. These were the people this was really all about; his closest bros from the local surf scene with their flannel shirts and sleeve tattoos. It was the same crew that had been there when the band first got together. Back when Greg was still in high school and his older brother, Tim, was playing guitar and calling the shots. More than twenty years later, Greg was still playing the same old songs in front of the same old crowd. It hardly seemed worth all the effort these days.

The door swung open. Junior stood there in a plaid Catholic schoolgirl skirt that clung to her curves. Knee-high leather boots and a tattered BCC T-shirt completed the ensemble. Her hair was jet black and parted down the middle, long ponytails snaking down her neck. Greg liked that Junior still dressed up for the shows she booked. It reminded him of the girl he fell for in high school, not the single mom in sweats he sometimes ran into at the grocery store these days.

She parted ruby-red lips to scream at Greg.

"Showtime, old man!"

He watched the rest of the band climb up onto the stage in the background. The crowd cheered as they assumed their positions, Marco banging out a quick fill on the snare drum while Chris tuned up. Greg tried to squeeze by Junior, but she stuck out an arm.

"Somebody broke the mirror back here. Seems like a pretty pathetic rock star maneuver."

"I was mad about the green M&Ms. Nice shirt by the way."

She looked down at her chest, feigning surprise at the Bad Citizen Corporation logo.

"This old thing? I got it as a souvenir when I slept with the singer."

"You must have made an impression."

"I'm glad one of us did."

Junior smiled, holding up a pinky finger as Greg brushed by. He pushed his way through a gaggle of Hollywood wannabes, bounding up the stairs to the stage. Chris flashed a shit-eating grin while JJ nodded. Jerry remained facing his amp, ignoring Greg as he passed by.

Marco counted off the first song. Greg focused on his shirtless drummer as the band unleashed a wall of sound. He noticed for the first time that Marco had gotten a little soft around the middle now that he was eating regularly.

Greg waited for the intro to unwind before leaping at the mic stand. A furious flood of lyrics flowed from between gritted teeth as he searched the sea of over-dressed strangers in front of him. The band was near the end of their second song when Greg looked over at Chris. The kid's legs were planted in a wide stance, eyes fixed on the low-slung guitar before him. Long bangs flopped across his face, lips pinched into a painful grimace. Greg wasn't much older than him when he started playing in this band.

Cheering erupted when they took a break after the sixth song, but it was a little too polite for Greg's tastes. The fact that people could stand in front with their arms folded told him something was wrong. He couldn't remember the last show they played where there weren't at least a few people slamming. But tonight it felt more like a recital, and it only fueled his anger.

He went to the edge of the stage, crouching down to shout.

"Have you pussies seen any of my friends? They look more like me than you."

He was pointing at them now, jabbing his finger only inches from stunned faces in the front row. There was some screaming from the back of the room and a few people laughed, but nobody moved.

"What the hell are you doing here tonight anyway? You get lost on your way to the farmers' market?"

A few people in front took a step back, but it wasn't nearly the reaction Greg wanted. He was ready to jump down there with them when Chris tore into the opening riff of the next song. Greg had no choice but to sing as they pounded out five more in quick succession, each one a little faster than the last. And when they stopped, it was more of the same.

"You guys slumming it in North Bay tonight?"

A few people clapped while others booed.

"That's more like it…"

Greg spun around to face Marco. He was clutching the microphone so tightly in his fist that blood oozed from the cuts again. Thin red strings ran down his fingers and along his forearm.

"Let's get this show over with so we can send these fuckers home."

Marco lifted his sticks, clicking off the next set. It was every song on side one of the first BCC album, in order. A blistering ten minutes of pure, youthful rage that left the band in tatters when the show finally ended. Greg knew it wasn't the best gig they'd ever played, but it wasn't bad for a bunch of old men, a hired gun, and a thirteen-year-old kid.

Greg went straight down the steps, making a beeline for the storage closet. Somebody caught his arm. He was still buzzing from the show and anxious for a little alone time, so he didn't appreciate the sudden intrusion. His first instinct was to rear back and take a swing, which he might have done if it wasn't Junior. He knew that was a fight he probably wouldn't win.

"Who the hell are all of these people? I didn't recognize anybody."

"Of course not. Your record label bought most of the tickets before any of the locals had a chance. Everybody here is connected to the music business in some way. Or a tastemaker."

That last word looked like it left a sour taste in Junior's mouth. It made Greg feel queasy, too.

"Why the hell didn't you tell me?"

"Because I would have missed out on all of your witty stage banter. Come on, there are some people over at the bar who want to meet you."

Junior walked off before he could finish complaining. She led him through the crowd, winding their way over to the bar. Normally JJ would be back there mixing drinks, but he'd taken the night off to play the show. Greg spent so little time at Eddie's these days that he didn't even recognize the new bartender.

Two middle-aged guys stood from their barstools when Greg walked over. Their young arm candy didn't even bother looking up from their phones. The taller of the two men had a light English accent that could have been a put on. He was rock-star thin, with a shag haircut straight out of some eighties Rod Stewart music video. It went well with his flared jeans and slim leather coat.

"I'm Peter James. Impressive set."

Greg shook his hand while looking around for Junior. The producer went on talking, trying to get his attention.

"Dead March sent us down here to have a look at your show. They thought Mick and I might be a good fit to produce your album."

He slapped his partner on the shoulder, which seemed to wake him up.

"Sorry. Pulled an all-nighter with a new hip-hop act. Barely keeping it together right now. Nice to meet you."

Greg smiled dismissively before turning back to Peter.

"That's weird. Nobody told me you were coming."

"We weren't totally sure we could make it, to be honest. So they probably couldn't be bothered. Have you got any studios in mind for where you'd like to record?"

"Haven't given it much thought. We're mostly concentrating on the tour right now. It starts in a few days."

Greg gave the room another quick scan, desperate to see some familiar faces. Peter's arms were folded when he turned back. He seemed to be looking right through Greg. Probably considering his aura, or some other hippie crap Greg didn't believe in.

"Interesting…"

Greg was plotting his escape when Junior reappeared. She had two young women with her, both of them short, blonde, and dressed for an outdoor summer festival. Greg wondered if Eddie would even recognize his own bar if he walked in right then. Thankfully, the old man was officially retired these days and didn't bother with the shows any more.

Junior made the introductions.

"This is Lindsay and Shauna. They're from the PR firm working with your label."

Lindsay stepped forward until she was right under Greg's chin.

"You're actually taller than you look on stage. We loved your set, by the way. So *hardcore*."

"Uh, thanks. That's kind of our thing."

She released a high-pitched giggle, slapping at his chest. Her small hand practically suctioned to his sweat-soaked shirt before she pulled it free. Greg motioned to the dressing room before walking way.

"Nice meeting you guys. I really have to change."

"Go do your thing. We look forward to working with you."

The two girls waved in unison as Junior escorted him away.

"Get your stuff together. I'll meet you back over at the bar when you're ready."

"Like old times, huh?"

Junior winked and spun off. Greg watched her push a few stragglers toward the exit as she made her way across the mostly empty room. His high school girlfriend had somehow become the only constant in his life.

The door to the storage closet was already open a crack when Greg grabbed the knob. He pushed it inward, groping at the wall for the lights. His backpack was right where he left it, but something dangled above it now. It took him a second to make sense of the limp body hanging from the rafters.

A rope was around his neck; sign taped to his chest: "I am Tim."

Chapter 2

The Bay Cities police didn't let Greg leave Eddie's until almost three in the morning. He was exhausted when he finally got home, but couldn't sleep after what he'd seen. Visions of the lifeless body filled his mind whenever he closed his eyes. His stomach dropped when he pictured the sign around the victim's neck.

Greg was so lost in his sleep-deprived haze that he almost forgot Marco was there, until he heard his voice.

"You doing okay, bro?"

"What? Yeah. Finding that kid at the club last night screwed with my head."

"Go easy on yourself. There's nothing you could have done."

"I think I'm through saving people, Marco. But why couldn't somebody else find the body for a change?"

Greg was thankful that his friend didn't respond. He just wanted to put the whole thing behind him and move on with his life. Changing the subject was a good place to start.

"Hope you're ready for a busy day."

He and Marco planned to stop by the SUP Sober meeting down at the beach before getting back to work. There was still a lot of planning to do for the BCC tour, along with a few loose ends to tie up from their last case. The business partnership was still new, but seemed to be working out so far—even if they didn't agree on everything.

"Dude. I thought of a name for our PI firm. Came to me on stage last night."

"We already have a name."

"I know, I know. But check it out."

Marco flung his hands out, as if lighting the words up in neon when he spoke.

"Bad. Citizen. *Investigations*."

Greg groaned from where he stood at the stove.

"Let's stick with Salem and Associates."

"Why the hell do I always have to be *associates*?"

"Because I'm the one with the PI license."

Marco mumbled something under his breath as Greg shoveled bacon and eggs onto two plates.

"Holy shit. With all the insanity, I forgot to tell you we got a new job. Dude called me last night before the gig."

Greg slammed a plate down in front of Marco.

"Are you crazy? We're leaving on tour in a few days. We don't have time to take on a new case."

"It's a one-night stakeout. We take some pictures and—*boom*— we're out. Be nice to have some cash in the bank when we get back from playing those shows."

"This isn't going to be that kind of tour, Marco. We're getting pretty big guarantees from the venues, plus whatever money we make off of T-shirts. Call him back and say we can't do it."

Marco tore a fatty piece of bacon with his teeth, swigging coffee.

"Fine. I'll do it without you."

"Again. I'm the one with the license. You don't have to worry about money."

"No such thing as enough money, bro. Not when you're my age and don't have shit in your savings account."

Somebody knocked on the front door. The noise woke Kristen and the baby up. Both of them immediately started screaming from the bedroom.

Marco almost fell out of his seat at the sudden flurry of activity. He'd been a little jumpy since being held captive by a violent cult leader the previous year at Grizzly Flats. The scars all over his body were fading, but the trauma was still right below the surface.

"The fuck is going on around here? It's like a war zone."

"I'll give you three guesses."

Greg got up and walked over to the front window, sliding the curtains back to peek outside. Bay Cities Police Chief Robert Stanley stood there looking half asleep with a uniformed cop at his side. He was short and stocky, with a sharp jawline and a military buzz cut the color of driftwood. Freckles covered almost every inch of his tanned face and arms, as if he'd spent his whole life walking a beat.

They spotted Greg and motioned to the door in unison. He reached for the knob, pulling it open a few inches.

"Love your costume, but Halloween isn't for a few months."

The Police Chief forced a smile. Greg's old nemesis had dark circles under his eyes.

"Good morning, Mr. Salem. Mind if we come in?"

"I do, but I'm not sure it would stop you."

Greg swung the door open. Officer Bob immediately went for the kitchen table where Marco sat with his arms folded.

"Oh, good. You're both here. That'll make things easier."

Officer Bob poured himself a cup of coffee and took a seat. His partner stayed put just inside the door, casing the house with a skeptical look.

"Nice place. You buy it with all the money from the book that guy wrote about you?"

He motioned to the living room with a stiff nod. Greg glanced at the book on the coffee table. The one that set the BCC reunion in motion. A book called *Among the Grizzlies* that spent a few weeks on *The New York Times* bestseller list and featured several chapters about a certain punk singer turned disgraced police officer named Greg Salem. The author was his friend, Tommy Thompson, who had written a personalized inscription on the first page thanking Greg for "the story of a lifetime." That's as far as Greg had gotten in the book responsible for changing his life.

Greg dodged the question with one of his own.

"Who's your nosy friend, Officer Bob?"

"Sorry. Greg Salem, meet Detective Bowers. He recently joined us from Hollywood."

Marco coughed loudly into his fist. Officer Bob took the hint.

"And this is Mr. Salem's friend—"

"Associate."

"Sorry. This is Mr. Salem's *associate*, Marco Johnson. Are you still living out in the garage?"

"Hell no, we use that as an office now. JJ and I got a sick condo up in North Bay, right up the street from Eddie's. Fucking Jacuzzi on the roof and everything."

Greg and Detective Bowers came over to the table to sit down. Officer Bob quickly moved on from the small talk.

"Funny you should mention Eddie's..."

Greg leaned back in his chair.

"No shit. I thought you two were here for my world-famous pancakes."

It looked like Detective Bowers was about to smack the smile from Greg's face. Officer Bob stepped in before things could escalate.

"Take it easy, Bowers. This is a little dance we do. It's been like this since I taught him how to throw a curve ball in Little League. Isn't that right, Mr. Salem?"

"Almost blew my arm out when I was nine. Coach of the year."

Officer Bob escaped into his head for a minute. There was definitely something off about him, but Greg couldn't put his finger on it. His voice was raspier than usual, for one thing.

"I read the statement you gave my officers last night. I was wondering if you had anything to add, now that you've had some time to think it over?"

Visions of the dead body dangling from the ceiling flooded Greg's mind again. The kid looked to be in his early twenties, and dressed like any other skate punk from The Bay Cities with low-top sneakers, jeans, and a flannel shirt. He reminded Greg of a million guys from the beach he'd known over the years. *Hell, I probably went to high school with his father.*

The victim also made him think of Chris, who had tried to hang himself while in rehab the previous year. And Greg's brother, Tim, of course, thanks to the note. They found him in the same position next door to Eddie's almost twenty years before. It was his brother's punk rock record shop back then, but Junior's salon was the current tenant. Greg tried to shake the unwanted memories from his head.

"I told you everything I know. I was the one who found the body, but I've never seen him before. Were you guys able to make an ID?"

"Let us ask the questions. Tell us about the note."

Greg sensed Officer Bob was uncomfortable bringing it up. He was the one who'd ruled Tim's death a suicide all those years ago. Greg was still convinced his brother had been murdered.

"Don't tell me you're calling this a suicide, too?"

Officer Bob said nothing in response, so Detective Bowers jumped in.

"We'll make that determination once we have all the facts straight."

"Your 'facts' will prove this is a suicide if that's what you're searching for."

Detective Bowers slammed his hand down on the table.

"Answer the questions and—!"

Marco silenced him with a loud "*Shush.*"

"Keep it down, the baby's still asleep."

Officer Bob gave an understanding nod. Detective Bowers immediately started in on Greg again, his voice a few decibels lower.

"I don't care if that book made you famous, I don't care that you grew up around here, and I sure as hell don't give two shits that you used to be on the job. I want this case closed as soon as possible, so you better start answering our questions about the suicide."

Greg jumped up, his chair clattering to the floor.

"Who the hell goes to a club to kill themselves? It just doesn't make any sense."

The loud noise got the baby crying in the bedroom again. This time Kristen wandered in with their son in her arms. She looked like she hadn't slept in days.

"This is quite a party. What's going on in here?"

Marco got up to walk their unwanted guests out. Greg went over to calm Kristen down.

"I'll explain later. Take the baby back in the bedroom. I'll be there in a second."

Her tired eyes darted around the room.

"Is this about what happened at the show last night?"

"Yes, but these two were just leaving."

Officer Bob stood, motioning for Bowers to do the same.

"Sorry to get you out of bed."

The four of them went out onto the porch while Kristen pacified the baby on the couch. Marco's arms were down at his side, chest puffed out. The aggressive stance didn't go unnoticed by Detective Bowers. Things were getting tense when Greg stepped between them.

"You'll have to forgive my friend. He's a little protective of my family. And he's stressed out about our tour."

Detective Bowers shook his head, bringing his hands up to rest on his hips. His eyes went straight up to Greg's burgundy hair.

"Aren't you two a little old to be playing in a punk band?"

Marco snorted.

"Aren't you a little short to play the bad cop?"

Officer Bob nodded goodbye, leading his partner away. Greg watched them go, already disgusted by all the mistakes those two would make in this investigation. He kicked at the weeds poking up through the cracks in the sidewalk, waiting for them to drive off.

Marco was right at his side.

"What's up, bro?"

Greg shook his head.

"What if they're right?"

"About what?"

"About it being a suicide."

ৎ

IT WAS ALREADY A beautiful day at the beach. Flags on top of the lifeguard stand danced in a light breeze as Greg and Marco schlepped their paddleboards across the cold morning sand. Eddie was waiting for them at the shoreline when they arrived. The old man was a lot thinner now that he stopped drinking, and a lot happier since retiring from the bar business.

"Where the hell have you two been? It's getting late."

Eddie motioned to the mostly flat ocean behind him. The rest of the SUP Sober crew was already in the middle of their twelve-step meeting a few hundred yards out to sea. Marco dropped his board into the water, pushing into the light surf. Greg stayed back to speak with Eddie.

"Sorry. We had an unexpected meeting with Officer Bob."

Eddie squished his face into a look approximating concern.

"About last night?"

"I'm not sure what Junior told you, but I'm the one who found the body."

"Sorry, Greg. You doing okay?"

"I'm fine. I just wish Officer Bob and his new attack dog would do their job and leave me alone."

"Well, they probably won't be sniffing around for too long. The kid hung himself, case closed."

Greg's shoulder muscles went stiff. It was a little easier to hear Eddie jumping to conclusions than the BCPD, but not by much. He decided it wasn't worth an argument.

"You know Officer Bob. He never misses the chance to give me a hard time."

"I guess so, but you'd think that would change now that he's about to retire."

Greg almost dropped his board to the sand. He couldn't believe his ears.

"He's retiring? Since when?"

"Don't act so surprised. It's been coming for a while now. Come on, we have to get going."

Eddie paddled out with Greg right behind him. The water looked like glass as they glided along at a good clip. It took them no time to reach the others. Marco was ranting when they arrived. Sobriety was a familiar subject matter for Greg, but he liked that his friend was getting more comfortable talking about it around other people.

"I've done a lot of gnarly shit in my life, but nothing prepared me for killing that dude. It's like I relive that moment every time I close my eyes. And when I open them again, all I want to do is get wasted. Like, really fucking wasted."

They all nodded along in understanding, but nobody spoke in case he had more to say. A full minute passed before the group's leader, Pete, turned to welcome Greg and Eddie.

"Great to see you. We're getting ready to wrap it up, but I wanted to give you guys the chance to share. Want to start, Greg?"

Greg was still rattled by the last twenty-four hours. And he was stunned by the news about Officer Bob. The two of them had been battling each other for so many years that it felt like losing a limb. He couldn't imagine what life in The Bay Cities would be like without his nemesis around. He was a little annoyed that Officer Bob didn't bother to mention it.

But his disappointment was nothing compared to the mounting dread he felt about going on tour. He was riddled with guilt about leaving Kristen and his son behind while he went out to relive his youth. And he worried a lot about what road life would do to Junior's son, Chris. That kid had already experienced a lot more loss than your average thirteen-year-old, and Greg was about to throw him into the deep end of the rock and roll cesspool.

Greg knew from experience that touring wasn't a lifestyle to be taken lightly. It'd turned most of his band into raging drug addicts the last time around, and transformed him into one of the most violent people on the planet. And now all of those familiar feelings were welling up inside of him again, fueled by everything that had torn his life to pieces in the twenty-something years since his last tour. *Is there a worse omen than finding a dead body back stage after your first show?*

It was enough to make him want to start drinking again, something on his mind a lot these days. The thought of everything he might lose made him want to vomit. Greg gripped the paddle in his hands until his knuckles went white.

He'd gone so deep into his own thoughts that he almost forgot he was bobbing on a paddleboard in the Pacific Ocean. He looked up, slowly realizing the rest of the group was still waiting for him to answer Pete's question.

"I'm good. I've got a lot going on right now, but everything's fine."

"Cool. How about you, Eddie?"

If Greg felt like his life was spinning out of control, Eddie was riding a wave of euphoria. He spent his mornings out on his paddleboard, his afternoons playing pool and shooting the breeze with a few of his friends at the bar, and most of his evenings with Junior and Chris. He'd even started dating again.

Seeing Eddie doing so well would normally make Greg happy, but these days it was too much to stomach. He waited until the old man got through the sunshine report before the three of them paddled back to shore together. Eddie said his goodbyes when they reached the beach. Greg turned to Marco.

"You ever worry about going back out on the road?"

"Hell yeah, dude. It's hard enough trying to stay clean around here where everybody's watching out for me. Who knows what the hell will happen once we get in the van."

"At least we can look out for each other."

"Totally. I'm looking forward to a little hang time with you, too, bro. Is Kristen pissed you're bailing?"

"She's always pissed about something these days, but she'll be fine while I'm gone. At least I hope so."

They walked another few yards across the sand before Marco broke the momentary silence.

"You think I'll ever find a chick to settle down with?"

"Of course. There has to be at least one woman out there crazy enough. You ever think about signing up for one of those online services?"

"Like a dating app?"

"I was thinking more like a mail-order bride."

"Hilarious, bro."

Greg stopped laughing when he spotted a familiar figure in the distance, leaning against a cinderblock wall. His pressed jeans and long-sleeved shirt were hard to miss at the beach, but Greg couldn't take his eyes off the blue hat.

The sun shined directly in Greg's face, but he'd recognize that face anywhere. His cheeks had filled out a little since the last time they spoke, and there was a wispy mustache on his upper lip now—like his older brother's. Greg wondered if it really was the kid who cost him his badge and haunted his dreams.

Whoever it was stood there watching Greg and Marco for a few more moments, before disappearing around the nearest corner and out of sight.

"Did you see that, Marco?"

"See what, bro?"

Greg decided to make a phone call the minute he got home.

◈

"Hey, Chief. It's me."

There was a long pause. Greg actually worried for a moment that his old Police Chief in Virgil Heights hung up on him. They hadn't really spoken in a few months, mostly because Greg kept finding reasons not to call. This wasn't just his old mentor and boss, this was the man who finally got Greg sober after his brother died.

The response Greg finally got was a few degrees above freezing.

"How's the PI business?"

"Good. We've actually got a stake out later tonight."

"Like old times. What're you calling me for?"

"Nothing. Wanted to check in."

That one got a dismissive chuckle. It sounded like the Chief was working hard not to blow a gasket.

"Cut the crap, Greg. You only call when you need something."

"Come on, Chief. I'm—"

"Get to the point, I'm busy."

Greg took a deep breath. This wasn't how we wanted the call to start.

"Fine. I was wondering if you've heard anything about the kid, you know, since my last meeting with him?"

His question was met with a deep sigh. Greg braced himself. Whatever info the Police Chief had, it wasn't going to be good.

"You didn't hear? He got out last month, when he turned eighteen. Came home to live with his parents."

"So he's back in Virgil Heights…"

"Yes and no. The whole family moved right after—"

Greg felt a familiar rage rising up in his chest.

"You telling me you guys lost track of him?"

"Of course not. He's signed up with a trade program downtown. One of those non-profit halfway houses that rehab gangbangers. I've actually been mentoring him. Why do you ask?"

There was no good answer to his question, but Greg knew he had to come up with something. In the end he decided on the truth since the Chief had already seen Greg at his absolute worst.

"I thought I saw him today, down here at the beach."

"I suppose that's possible. He's got a parole officer, but he's free to come and go as long as he keeps his nose clean. And you don't have a restraining order…"

"So he's free to lurk around my neighborhood, making me feel uncomfortable?"

The line went silent again after Greg's explosive response, but only for a second. The Police Chief's voice tinged with a familiar concern now.

"I wouldn't worry if I were you. From what I can tell he's on the straight and narrow. I'd be willing to bet it wasn't even him."

"How can you be so sure?"

"He's changed. I don't know how else to explain it."

Greg was dazed when they said their goodbyes and hung up.
He went into the bathroom, took out his clippers, and shaved his hair
down to a buzz cut. Small patches of dye still clung to the tips of the
inch-long strands, but his natural blond was already poking through.
It was time to get to work.

Chapter 3

They sat in a darkened car high up on the peninsula a few hours later. It was a non-descript compact number that Greg bought Marco for exactly this purpose. His baby blue El Camino would stick out like a sore thumb among the Range Rovers and Teslas the valets were lining up along the driveway. And he wasn't willing to risk having his precious ride get banged up again after all the time and money he'd spent to restore her.

The stake out had just begun, but Greg was ready to call it quits. He was behind the wheel with Marco in the passenger seat. The ornate fences of enormous homes lined the narrow road on either side of them, creating a canyon of brick, ivy, and wrought iron winding down for a couple of miles to the cliffs above the tidal pools. From there, the black ocean spread out in a panoramic view bordered by the twinkling lights of South Bay.

Greg and Marco were positioned across the street, hoping they looked like two more members of the Hollywood press. A camera bag was on the floor at Marco's feet, along with a file folder and a couple of empty energy drink cans.

The multi-million-dollar home they were watching was set a couple hundred yards back from the street. A circular, cobblestone driveway swooped across the rolling front lawn, delivering carloads of guests to the columned front porch. A throng of paparazzi was stationed outside on the street, hoping to catch a glimpse of anybody from the exclusive guest list.

"Are all of these vultures here for our girl?"

"Not really sure. The dude told me she was some kind of musician, but I've never heard of her before."

"Glad you did your homework. You're a total pro."

"You've got a computer, too, boss."

"What's her name again?"

"Gabriella Flores."

They had a clear view of the valet stand and front door, as well as one side of the house. A DJ was set up in the backyard, the beams of an elaborate light show causing the night sky to pulsate with color. The low-end from the DJ's speakers was so loud that the dashboard in front of Greg and Marco vibrated in time to the electronic dance music.

Greg almost had to scream to be heard.

"How they hell do they listen to this crap?"

Marco snorted.

"That's what our parents used to say about punk rock."

Greg reached over to give his partner a solid punch on the thigh. Marco jumped up in his seat, ramming his stringy blond hair into the roof of the car.

"What the fuck, dude? That hurt!"

"Be quiet. Those leeches across the street will hear you."

"What's a matter, bro? Afraid they'll want to take your picture?"

Greg ignored him, checking the clock on his phone instead. They'd already been there for an hour without any sign of the woman they were trailing.

"Are you sure she's inside already?"

"For the millionth time, yes. The driver dropped her off. Chill out."

"This doesn't make any sense. Why are we trailing her if she has a driver?"

"I told you, her old man's paranoid. He thinks everybody's screwing her, including the driver. What do you care, anyway? It's easy money."

"There's no such thing as 'easy money.' What's her husband's name?"

"Hell if I know. Some lawyer set this whole thing up. Said she's totally out of control, doing blow and hooking up with all these random dudes. Or at least that's what they think she's up to, so they're looking for proof."

"Does this lawyer have a name?"

"I think it's Torres, or something like that. Maybe Trujillo?"

"Once again, that's some solid detective work."

"What the hell's your problem? I'm trying to make some extra cash here."

"I don't know. There's something off about this whole situation."

"Maybe that's what happens when an old guy marries some hot young chick."

Marco smiled, arching an eyebrow. Greg didn't find it funny at all.

"Kristen isn't that much younger than me. Besides, what the hell would you know about—"

Greg didn't have the chance to finish his come back. Marco started banging on the dashboard and pointing toward the house.

"There she is. Getting into that car with those two dudes."

"You sure?"

Greg squinted to take a closer look. She was medium height with straight black hair that bounced and swung as she stumbled toward the car. Her form-fitting white dress seemed to glow in the darkness, calling attention to her killer curves. Marco reached down and grabbed a black-and-white headshot from the file folder at his feet. He looked from the glossy image to the girl in the driveway a few times before making up his mind.

"That's totally her."

"Quit acting like she's an old friend of yours."

"She might as well be, as much as I've been staring at this picture."

Greg turned the key in the ignition, but left the headlights off. An expensive European sports car shot from the driveway a moment later and tore off down the street. He counted to three in his head before putting Marco's car into drive to give chase. They'd gone half a block before he flipped the lights on.

It was late at night and there weren't many streetlights in the secluded, hilltop neighborhood. Greg gave his prey plenty of distance.

He kept his eyes focused on the red brake lights blinking and flashing in front of him as they sped along the serpentine streets. A few minutes passed before the two cars encountered their first stoplight. Greg eased his car to the curb two blocks back, waiting until the light turned green and the sports car went left.

Greg stepped on the gas, barely making the quick-changing light as Marco screamed "Go! Go! Go!" The sports car was reduced to a couple of small red dots in the distance as they sped along the desolate four-lane boulevard connecting South Bay with the grungy harbor town on the other side of the hill. In between were ten miles of winding roads where local teens came to race the souped-up cars and motorcycles their wealthy parents bought them. But nobody else was around on a school night.

The only sign of life was a high-end golf resort called The Cliffs that locals treated like a private country club. The sports car barely tapped the brakes before screeching into the driveway and skidding to a stop outside the lobby. Greg killed his headlights and pulled over, watching as both doors flung open. The two men climbed out, pushing the passenger seat forward to help their guest up. The driver tossed his keys to the valet and they each took an arm to lead Gabriella inside, practically holding her up.

Marco tried to open his door, but Greg stopped him.

"Where are you going?"

"This whole scene's sketchy. We have to stop those dudes before they get her into their hotel room."

"Hold on. The lawyer told you she slept around, which is exactly what this looks like to me. We can't go around kicking doors in."

Marco sat back with a groan.

"Whatever. You know you aren't a cop anymore, right?"

"That's my point. We don't have badges and, from what I saw, there's nothing illegal going on."

"She seemed kind of wasted."

"People get wasted and fuck all the time. That's how we got this job in the first place, right? Speaking of which…"

Greg grabbed the camera from the floor at Marco's feet and started snapping pictures. He had more than enough evidence to collect a check before the trio disappeared.

"Now we wait for them to come back out. Might be a while from the looks of things."

Greg reached over to turn on the radio. He tuned it to an AM news station that ran through the day's headlines. Greg felt a sense of relief these days whenever he didn't hear his own name mentioned.

Marco, on the other hand, still seemed pretty annoyed.

"Can you at least play some music?"

"In a minute. I want to catch the surf report."

Greg turned the car stereo's dial back and forth, trying to pick up a clean signal. Marco sighed.

"You think it'll be weird for us to go on tour without Tim?"

Greg stopped twirling the dial long enough to look up.

"What the hell made you think of that?"

"I don't know, bro. The whole thing feels fucked up. Like maybe we shouldn't be messing with ancient history, or something. Out of respect for your brother."

Greg went back to tuning the radio, but not before putting an end to the conversation.

"It's just music. Tim's dead and he isn't coming back. Take a nap or something."

Marco swung the passenger door open to step out.

"Whatever, bro. I need to piss."

"Fine. You know where to find me."

Marco slammed the door, and for a brief moment the station broke through the static.

"...*speaking about his new book,* Among the Grizzlies. *Thanks for joining us today, Mr. Thompson...*"

Greg sat back, waiting to hear his friend's voice.

"*Thanks for having me.*"

"*This is quite a book you've written about your time undercover with a drug cult in the Angeles National Forest. A* New York Times *bestseller, I might add. When did you know you had such an exciting story on your hands?"*

"It's hard to say. I'd been chasing after Tom Schulte—"

"The drug kingpin better known as 'Magnus Ursus.' Did he really call himself that?"

"Yep. I'd been keeping an eye on Magnus and his crew, hanging out at the biker bar up near their camp—"

"Grizzly Flats."

"Wow. I'm impressed you actually read the book. I was looking for a way in when they kidnapped a couple of hikers. One of them turned out to be a former police officer and punk musician named Greg Salem..."

Greg changed the station the second he heard his own name. He turned to the right to say something to Marco, realizing too late that his partner had been gone for a while. Greg looked out the windshield to the lobby. Marco walked through the front doors, turning in the same direction as Gabriella Flores and her two escorts.

He slammed his hands against the steering wheel before reaching over to grab his Glock from the glove compartment. Gun in hand, he flung the door open and jumped out. He started off jogging, but slowed to a fast walk when he passed by the valet stand. There was no sign of Marco when Greg got inside. He scanned the small crowd gathered around a piano bar in the lounge, drunkenly singing along to a Neil Diamond song. His eyes wandered through the window to an enormous pool glowing blue in the darkness outside.

Greg headed for the restaurant, catching a glimpse of Marco between two closing elevator doors. He ran over to catch him, but didn't make it in time. Greg watched closely as the floor lights counted up from "L" to "4" before stopping. He slammed through the stairwell door, climbing the steps two at a time.

He was winded when he exited into a long hallway a minute later. There were a couple of antique chairs and a small wooden table near a window on his right. Ornate mirrors and paintings lined the walls between the guest room doors. And there was Marco at the far end, his ear against a door and his hand on the knob.

Greg hissed at his partner as he approached.

"What the hell are you doing?"

Marco brought a finger up to his lips, signaling for Greg to be quiet. He motioned to the room with his head.

"They took her in there."

"So what? She went with them on her own. There's nothing we can do about it."

Greg reached out to pull Marco back, but his friend wouldn't budge.

"Something's not right, bro. I know it."

That's when Gabriella started screaming. It sounded like it might be laughter at first, but it quickly evolved into sheer terror. And then they heard her shout, "Help!"

Greg shoved Marco aside, stepping back to give the door a solid kick. It crashed inward with a spray of splinters.

He stormed in with his gun raised, sweeping it back and forth to cover the room. The two guys were bent over a nightstand covered in coke. One had floppy blond hair and the other dark curls. They were taking turns with a rolled up hundred-dollar bill. Both of them wore tight-fitting underwear that barely concealed their rock-hard erections. Gabriella was naked on the mattress, wrists tied to the bedposts. Tears streamed down her cheeks as Marco rushed over to set her free.

Greg kept his gun trained on the two men. They looked like a couple of frat boys from one of the private colleges downtown.

"Having a little party in here?"

"This was all her idea, I swear," said the blond.

"But then she started freaking out," added the other one.

"Lie to me again and I'll blow your dicks off."

Greg lowered the gun for emphasis. Marco lifted Gabriella off of the bed to help her find her clothes and purse. They were scattered across the room in a crooked line ending near the door.

She went into the bathroom to get dressed. Marco came over to join Greg, pointing at the two terrified men standing before him.

"What're we going to do with these idiots?"

"Get them on the bed and tie them up."

Marco did as he was told. He made each of them put both hands through one of the ropes on the bedpost. He secured the knots, pulling them tight until they dug into their wrists. Satisfied they wouldn't be going anywhere, he took a pinch of cocaine off the nightstand and threw it into their faces. The white powder clung to their eyelashes and sprinkled their cheeks.

Greg took his phone out and started snapping pictures. Then he went over to where their pants were piled up on the floor. He fished both driver's licenses out of their wallets, tucking them into his jeans.

"Now we know your names. And where you live. Tell anybody we were here and we'll hunt you down."

Marco laughed. He absentmindedly lifted his fingers up to lick them clean before Greg stopped him.

"Go wash that crap off your hands."

"Sorry, bro. Old habits die hard."

Marco passed by Gabriella, who'd wandered back into the room. She came over to stand next to Greg, a dazed look on her face. Her hair was perfectly tousled, and it looked like she'd touched up her lipstick. It was hard to believe she'd been screaming bloody murder a few minutes before.

"You guys literally saved my ass from these two."

An edge crept into her breathy voice, a hint of street smarts under the polished trophy wife façade. Greg shook his head.

"You can thank my friend. He's the hero tonight."

Gabriella looked over her shoulder toward the bathroom. Her face was only a few inches from Greg's when she looked back. He could smell fresh toothpaste on her breath, saw the light trapped in her amber eyes.

"Maybe I will."

Greg blinked first.

"Let's get out of here. I'll call the police from the car."

She shook her head with a dramatic pout.

"No cops. Let's just leave these jokers for hotel security to deal with. But first…"

She sprang, bounding across the bed until she was on top of the blond.

"Look at me, asshole!"

He squealed as she dragged her fingernails down the length of his cheek, digging jagged red cuts into his skin. His screams turned to sobs as she slowly backed away. It was as if nothing had happened by the time she reached Greg again. She straightened out her dress, spinning for the door.

"Ready when you are."

ჲ

GREG WAITED UNTIL THEY had her safely in Marco's car before he called in an anonymous tip to the desk clerk.

"A couple of coked up lunatics are trying to kill each other in the room next to mine..."

Greg was behind the wheel again, with Gabriella beside him. Marco held down the back seat as they flipped a U-turn and headed back toward the party where this all started. They'd only driven a couple of miles before she leaned a little closer to Greg.

"Let me guess. You guys work for my husband, right?"

"That obvious?"

She brought a finger up to twirl the ends of her hair. The frat boy's blood glistened on the tips of her nails.

"You can't take me home. He'll kill me. He'd probably kill all three of us."

Greg looked into the rearview mirror while she spoke, trying to make eye contact with Marco. He worried that this wouldn't turn out to be your average jealous husband case. Marco was busy looking out the window, lost in his own thoughts.

That left Greg on his own.

"I think we'll be fine. Not sure I can say the same for you."

She choked up a laugh that caught in her throat.

"You don't know shit about me."

"You're right, but it sounds like your husband's a powerful man. And he's getting tired of you screwing around behind his back."

"I get it. You're like some white knight, come to take the whore queen back to the king for her punishment. That it?"

"I honestly don't care who you screw, or who you screw over. This is just a job for me."

Her eyes were glassy with tears.

"Let me out here then. I can take care of myself."

Greg pulled over, calling her bluff. The sudden deceleration snapped Marco out of his trance.

"She can stay with me tonight. I'll take her home in the morning."

Greg couldn't believe his ears.

"Get real, Marco. Your place is a pig sty."

"Good point. Then she can stay in the office at your house. I'll text the lawyer to let him know what's up."

Chapter 4

*T*he kid in the blue hat had a gun in his outstretched hand, the tip of the barrel pressed firmly against Greg's temple. He gritted his teeth, sweat snaking down his face to the rope around his neck. He waited for the bullet that never came, praying for an end to all the promises of violence. Ready for the score to be settled at last. He heard the kid squeeze the trigger and felt the side of his head explode.

"WAKE. UP."

Greg forced his eyes open. Kristen stood there, their son in the crook of one arm. She slapped the side of his head with her free hand.

"Get out of bed right now."

He sat up, holding his head in his hands. His voice felt thick in his throat.

"What's going on?"

"There's somebody at the back door asking for you. Some woman in a slinky dress. It looks like she came here straight from clubbing."

Gabriella.

His mind flooded with memories of her naked body tied to the bedposts. He immediately tried to drive the images from his head. Not only because his wife was standing right over him, but because Gabriella was trouble. He knew it from the moment he laid eyes on her.

"Let me explain."

"Is this how it's going to be when you're on tour, Greg? Staying out all night with strange women while your son and I are stuck at home?"

"She's just a client with a violent husband. I let her sleep out in the garage last night."

It clearly wasn't the explanation Kristen hoped for. Either that or she could read his mind. She turned and stormed out without another word. Greg wanted to chase after her, but his head was still groggy from sleep. He stood up and staggered into the bathroom instead. The reflection in the mirror was the same one he'd tried to destroy at Eddie's, but now he saw something else there, too—the dull look of resignation that claimed his father's face in the last years of his life. The same gray cloud that crept behind his brother Tim's eyes when he gave into his addiction; utter hopelessness consuming him in the weeks before he died.

Greg didn't bother breaking the mirror this time. He was too tired and couldn't see the point. So he slipped into a pair of board shorts instead, zipping on a hoodie.

Kristen stayed on the couch when he walked through the living room. One side of her thick, green robe pulled open to feed their son. Her legs were folded beneath her as she stared down at her baby, pure love in her eyes. He watched Timmy's mouth as it sucked greedily, his little fist resting on his mother's chest. The body that once gave Greg so much pleasure had evolved into something much more vital. So beautiful that he wasn't sure he could ever bear to touch her again.

The pounding on the back door reminded him of what he was supposed to be doing. He slipped through the kitchen and out onto the deck. Gabriella reclined in a lounge chair, a forearm over her closed eyes. One knee was bent, forcing the hem of her dress to ride up. Greg found it hard to look away.

Her voice was low and smoky.

"You gonna offer me some coffee, or keep trying to figure out if I'm wearing underwear?"

"Sorry. Just making sure you were all right."

"Come on, Greg. You know I'm perfect."

She swung her legs to the deck, propping herself up. Now it was her turn to do the staring.

"The ocean sure does something to the bodies of you surfer boys."

He looked down in feigned surprise, giving his abs a pat. She stood up and straightened out her dress.

"Coffee?"

"Uh, yeah. Wait here. You take cream?"

"Whatever will make this hangover go away."

Greg was already heading inside, but she kept talking.

"You should probably get some coffee for your friend, too."

He stopped, watching her expression in the reflection of a window.

"Marco? He probably won't be here for another hour or so."

She cocked a hip, nodding to the garage.

"Last I checked he was still asleep. Believe me, I would know."

Greg turned around slowly, trying to wrap his head around what he heard. He prayed Marco hadn't made such an impossibly stupid mistake, but knew in his bones that he had. Why would she lie about something like this?

"I watched him drive away after we got out of the car."

"Well, he came back. And stayed all night. You jealous?"

The blood rushed up into his face as he tore across the backyard and into the garage.

"Get up, Marco. Now!"

His partner didn't budge, so Greg stomped over and slapped him across the head. Marco leapt up. His body pulsated with a burst of manic energy that made him look like a shaved monkey.

"Come at me, bro!"

Greg had no time for empty threats.

"Tell me you didn't do it."

"Do what?"

"Take a case to trail some guy's cheating wife and then end up sleeping with her yourself."

Marco's shoulders slumped as he collapsed down onto the pillows. Greg had his answer, but he couldn't let it go.

"Are you a fucking idiot? She stayed here last night because she was afraid her husband might kill her. Might kill all three of us."

"I know. It's—"

"A suicide mission? I already rescued you once. I'm not itching to do it again."

Marco pleaded for understanding.

"Look at that body, bro. I never stand a chance with chicks like her."

Greg didn't want to admit it, but he definitely understood. He'd made far worse decisions with women who ended up ruining his life in one way or another. But this time was different, mainly because it was Marco instead of him. *Come to think of it, maybe I am a little jealous.*

"Get dressed. We've got a huge mess to clean up."

֍

GREG SPED ALONG THE coast as Gabriella sat in the passenger seat with a scowl on her face. He couldn't tell if she hated the music or the way the wind made a mess of her hair. The sun was up in the sky and the smell of salt water swirled all around them. He had the El Camino's windows down and the stereo turned up. TSOL's "Code Blue" came on, but he hit forward before the chorus. The next track was "Institutionalized" by Suicidal Tendencies. Greg rolled up his window so she could hear him over the roar of the engine.

"What's the matter, don't like punk rock?"

She turned to face him, rolling her eyes.

"It all sounds exactly the same. It's boring as fuck."

"I could say the same thing about the dance trash you probably listen to."

"Whatever, old man. I'm into hip-hop anyway. The real shit, like you even know what that is."

"Give me a little credit. You're talking about The Beastie Boys and Eminem, right?"

Even she cracked a smile at that one.

"A lot has happened in music since you graduated college. How old are you anyway?"

"Same age as Marco."

He thought that might shut her up, but she came right back at him.

"Well at least he fucks like he's young."

Greg followed the road to the right, driving up along the cliffs. It was a clear day and he could see Catalina Island in the distance out the passenger window. Sparkling sunlight danced off of the ocean in between, creating a warm glow that softened Gabriella's hard edges.

"Why don't you leave your husband instead of cheating all the time?" She shot daggers.

"It's not that easy. You don't just leave Tony Flores. Besides, he does plenty of screwing around on his own. Ask his ex-wife if you don't believe me."

Tony Flores. It sounded familiar to Greg, but he couldn't place it.

"How'd you two meet?

"He signed me to his record label. Make a left up here."

Greg followed her detailed directions for the next couple of miles, navigating a maze of streets specifically designed to keep people like him out of this neighborhood. She finally told him to pull over when they reached the end of a cul de sac.

"It's *that* one."

The house she pointed to looked like something from a gangster rap video. Not exactly a mansion, but much bigger than anything Greg was used to. It must have been at least eight thousand square feet, judging by the enormous façade, with a star-shaped fountain in the circular driveway. A mobile car washing team was out there at the moment, carefully detailing several already shiny luxury cars. To top it all off, a helicopter sat on the enormous front lawn.

Greg almost couldn't believe people actually lived like this only a few miles from his own house.

"Need me to walk you in?"

She groaned dismissively, swinging the door open.

"Thanks, but no thanks. It's gonna to be hard enough getting through the jackals without explaining who you are."

Greg looked over to the front gate. A few cameramen were milling around outside.

"They here for you?"

"I wish. Tony's got a studio in the pool house where he records a lot of Latina pop stars. Where those girls go, these scumbags go. Thanks for the ride."

Gabriella climbed out, slamming the door. He watched her walk across the street, pushing through the small crowd of sleazy reporters. The engine revved and his hands were on the wheel when he noticed her purse on the seat next to him. He jumped out, calling her name.

She stopped and turned around. He held the purse up, jogging over to give it to her. It'd barely touched her outstretched hand when the cameras started going off. Greg froze for a split second before realizing he needed to get the hell out of there. He sprinted back over to the El Camino, threw it in drive and sped off.

৯

GREG GOT BACK TO South Bay thirty minutes later, thankful he still had most of the day to finish planning the tour. Unfortunately, a BCPD cruiser waited for him in his usual parking spot out back. Greg and his unexpected guest climbed out of their cars at the same time.

"Sorry to drop in unannounced."

"Kinda seems like your MO."

"Watch your mouth, smartass."

"What do you want?"

Detective Bowers pulled out a leather-bound notepad and flipped a few pages.

"I'll cut to the chase. We got a little more information about the victim from the club—"

"I don't want to know his name."

"Too bad. It's Tim Granger. Sound familiar?"

Greg folded his arms across his chest.

"Nope."

"We searched his apartment over in North Bay. He was a big fan of your band, had posters all over the walls and a few of your albums. What are you guys called again?"

"Bad Citizen Corporation. Where's Officer Bob?"

"Busy. Let's step inside. I have a few more questions to ask you."

Greg opened the back gate and motioned for him to take a seat at the patio table. He could hear the baby crying inside of the house, like always.

"Make it quick."

"I understand you've had some problems with your fans in the past. I read something about a BCPD parking enforcement officer in your file."

"'Some problems' would be a huge understatement. But it sounds like you know all about me. I need to get inside to help my wife."

"Have you read the book your friend wrote about you?"

"No. Why?"

"We found a copy at Mr. Granger's apartment. Several of the pages about you and your brother were bookmarked."

Detective Bowers pushed the chair back, stood up and went to the back gate.

"I'll have to listen to your band one of these days. Might help me understand why everybody around here thinks you're such a big deal."

Chapter 5

The rehearsal space smelled like dirty socks and fresh skunk. Greg left the roll-up door wide open for as long as he could, but they eventually had to close it to play at full volume. It turns out their new guitarist, Jerry, was a secret stoner and terrible at hiding it. His tight-fitting clothes reeked from the moment he arrived, and the pungent odor always lingered for a while after he left. Greg couldn't imagine how potent his stash must be, but judging by the vacant look on his long face and permanently red eyes, he guessed it must be practically lethal.

This presented an interesting challenge for the rest of the band, all of whom were clean and sober—including Chris, at the tender age of thirteen. Even JJ had sworn off weed, which was nothing short of a miracle. Worse than creating temptation, the smell reminded both Greg and Marco of the time they had spent at Grizzly Flats. Those memories were still too new—and the scars too fresh—for either of them to want to relive them. Even for a cheap contact high.

So Greg did his best to ignore Jerry and focus on the music, which came with its own ghosts. Not much had changed in the rehearsal space since he inherited it from his dead friend, Ricky. It was hard for him not to think of the time the two of them spent there together, but nobody haunted the BCC catalog quite like Greg's older brother, Tim. He formed the band back when Greg was still a kid. And he was the one who wrote most of the songs the band would be playing on this upcoming tour.

Greg started to wonder if there would be enough room in the van for all of the band members, living and dead. The flood of flashbacks had him pacing before they'd even started the first song of their last pre-tour rehearsal. From there, they'd run the set two or three times, or until the blisters on Marco's hands burned too bad for him to hold his sticks. That moment couldn't come soon enough for Greg most days, even though he was the one insisting they practice so often. *I'm the face of this band, and I really don't want to look like an asshole on stage.*

He pulled the microphone to his gritted teeth.

"Are we going to play any music tonight? Count us in."

They all played facing each other in a small circle, so Greg lifted his eyes to look at Marco. His drummer was busy wrapping thin strips of duct tape around his mangled fingers.

"Give me a second, bro."

"We've already been here almost an hour."

Greg heard his angry voice thundering from the PA, but couldn't bring himself to care. This tour would be challenging enough with everything else he had going on. He didn't want to embarrass himself on top of it by fronting a crappy band.

"Why don't you wear those drummer gloves?"

Marco looked up, pure horror on his face.

"Um. Because I'm not some heavy metal dirt bag?"

"Good answer. Just making sure you aren't going soft on me. Can we start now?"

Marco grabbed his sticks, bringing them up to click off the first song on the set list. Chris came in with the guitar a beat too early and everything immediately ground to a halt. Jerry slapped JJ on the shoulder.

"Last I checked, the band comes in after the four. Unless something changed."

Jerry was a thirty-something hired gun who'd toured or recorded with tons of major punk bands over the last decade. His spiky hair was dyed platinum blond, making his different colored eyes—one blue, one hazel—seem to glow in contrast. What he lacked in personality, he more than made up for in raw talent.

JJ shrugged him off, turning to face Chris.

"This one's a little tricky. No need to rush. Hang back and you'll get it."

Jerry stepped over to the nearest mic, his eyes on Chris.

"Nothing tricky about it. Wait until Marco counts to four and then come in. You know how to count, right?"

Greg tried letting the scene play out, but he'd finally had enough. He wanted to leave no doubt whose band this was.

"Chris, come in after the four. Got it? Jerry, stop being a dick. Marco, let's try it again."

Marco did as he was told. He'd clicked three out of four times when somebody started banging on the metal door. Greg cursed into the microphone while Chris took his guitar off and went to open up. Most teenage boys on the verge of rocking out would be disappointed to find their mom standing there, but not Chris.

"Did you bring us dinner?"

Junior stepped inside, immediately pulling a face.

"It smells like ass in here."

Marco set his sticks down on the snare drum. The rest of the band took their instruments off in turn. Junior handed two heaping bags of fast food and a drink caddy to her son before shooing him off. She joined Greg at the back of the room while the rest of the band shoveled fries into their faces. He noticed that her retro punk outfit from the other night had been replaced by the usual baggy sweatshirt, blue jeans, and flip-flops.

"How's it going tonight, rock star?"

"You got here in the nick of time. It actually looked like we might play a song for a second there."

"Don't blame me if you guys don't move as fast as you used to. Besides, I'm not letting my kid starve so you can indulge a midlife crisis."

Junior always had a way of making Greg smile.

"How will he survive on the road without you?"

"He won't have to. I decided I'm coming with you guys."

Junior folded her arms to signal that there wouldn't be any discussion about it. Greg brought his voice down to a whisper.

"I must finally be going deaf because I didn't understand a word you just said."

"Read my lips—he's just a kid."

"And he'll be in a van full of his favorite uncles."

"Exactly. No way I'm trusting you losers with my only child."

"The label already found us a tour manager. Some woman that handles most of their major acts."

Junior's eyes flooded with rage.

"I'm not coming to work for you. I'm coming to watch out for my son. End of story."

Greg took a step back, raising his arms in surrender. Junior looked shocked.

"Wow. That was a little too easy. You're getting soft in your old age."

"No time for arguments. Besides, I know when I'm beat."

"Well, I hope you're doing okay. Anything I can help with?"

"It would be awesome if you kept me from finding any more dead bodies."

"You're on your own there."

Junior gave a nervous giggle. Greg thought it was out of character for her, but also totally out of line given the situation. His blood began to boil.

"It wasn't so funny when your son tried to hang himself last year."

Chris walked over, right on queue. He was a big kid, only a few inches shorter than Greg these days. His hair was dyed black and shaved to a uniform length on most of his head, except for long bangs shielding his eyes from view. The peach fuzz mustache on his upper lip easily could have been residue from the chocolate milkshake in his right hand. A phone was in his left.

"What're you guys talking about?"

They both answered at the same time.

"Nothing," said Greg.

"The tour," said Junior.

Chris brought the straw up to his lips, taking a long pull. He swirled the thick, brown liquid around his mouth and swallowed.

"That's cool. I thought maybe you were talking about these pictures of Greg."

Chris held the phone up, showing them the screen. It was definitely Greg and it almost looked like he was holding hands with Gabriella Flores outside of her estate. He grabbed the phone from Chris's hand, scrolling up to the top of the page of the entertainment gossip website. His eyes bugged out of his head when he read the headline:

Are Greg Salem and Gabriella Flores An Item?

A late night at an exclusive house party apparently turned into a sleepover for these two, according to the Hollywood rumor mill. Nobody remembers seeing punk hunk Greg Salem at the snazzy shindig, but it was hard to miss him when he brought luscious Latina rapper Gabriella Flores home the next morning. She still wore the same white dress as the night before, but her hair was a mess and she couldn't stop smiling. This wouldn't be the first time Grabby Gabby has cheated on her husband, superstar producer Tony Flores...

"Damn it!"

Greg shoved the phone back into Chris's palm before tearing off through the rehearsal space. He knocked a cheeseburger out of JJ's hands as he rushed by on his way to the El Camino. The engine roared to life before Greg closed his door. He sped off down Bay Cities Boulevard toward home without even saying goodbye.

"I SHOULD HAVE KNOWN by the way you've been acting."

"Come on, Kristen. Those gossip sites make things up. Whatever will get the most clicks."

"Keep your voice down, Timmy's napping."

Greg took a tentative step forward. He drew a deep breath through his nose, trying to calm himself down.

"You have to believe me."

Kristen stepped back, disappointment filling her eyes.

"I don't know what to believe. You're different somehow. So distant, and *angry* all the time."

"I'm working hard so we can afford to live here. One of us has to keep the cash coming in."

It was *exactly* the wrong thing to say. Nothing sent Kristen through the roof quicker than him downplaying the difficulties of motherhood. Greg learned the hard way, but it didn't stop him from making the same mistakes over and over again.

Concerns she had about waking the baby up were apparently gone.

"How dare you. I stay here with your son while you run around town like some wannabe rock star, and you have the nerve to...to..."

Kristen balled her hands into fists, stomping her feet as she spoke. Greg actually found it a little adorable. Sexy even. He tried to control his facial expression so things wouldn't escalate any further.

In the end, the baby saved his ass. He decided to thank his son for that, one day when the boy was old enough to understand.

"I'll get him."

"Fuck you, Greg."

She stormed off for the nursery. Greg went out into the backyard to smell the ocean air and try to calm down. It wasn't working, so he headed for the garage instead. He thought maybe he'd play a few records, strum a little guitar. Something else caught his attention instead. It was on the desk where his bed used to be.

Greg walked over, sizing the book up as he approached. The picture on the cover featured a replica of the red-and-white California state flag. It was tilted on one end, but the grizzly bear at the center was filled in with green marijuana plants instead of brown fur. *Among the Grizzlies* emblazoned the top edge of the dust jacket, with "Tommy Thompson" near the bottom.

He reached down to pick it up, surprised as always at how much it weighed. Greg had lived at Grizzly Flats—experienced the scope and scale of the illegal growing operation—and came to understand the madness that drove its founder, Magnus Ursus. And he'd been to nearly every other place Magnus wandered both before and after, from porn shoots in the valley to a yacht moored in the harbor off the shores of The Bay Cities. Even with so much first-hand knowledge, he couldn't imagine how Tommy managed to write this many words on the subject.

Greg was about to find out. He flipped the cover open to the table of contents, skimming chapter titles. The first few looked to be background information about Magnus—"Raised in the Wild," "A Cub in the City," "Out of Hibernation"—the origin story of a madman. The narrative changed with chapter seven, "Wild in the Streets," no doubt in honor of the classic Circle Jerks song. He flipped through the pages until he spotted those words in context. His name started the first paragraph:

Greg Salem grew up along the sunny beaches of Southern California during the eighties and nineties, blissfully unaware of the man who would one day ruin his life. He and his older brother, Tim, killed time surfing the perfect break off of South Bay, skateboarding with friends in the parking lot of the local mall, and listening to the hardcore punk music that shaped their bad-boy image.

Bad-boy image? Greg got a laugh out of that line, even if he found it a little embarrassing. He had to force himself to keep reading.

Their neighborhood was home to a vibrant local music scene, inspired by legendary SoCal bands like Black Flag, Descendents, and Circle Jerks. One Bay Cities High School newspaper article from that era describes "bands practicing in every other garage along Bay Cities Boulevard," and unauthorized concerts at the local park's band shell— much to the consternation of local police. "They'd rip the locked cover off of the power outlets, plug in, and set up," said Bay Cities Police Chief, Robert Stanley. "I didn't really mind the music that much. Some of those kids were actually pretty talented, but a few of the residents in the nearby neighborhoods didn't agree with me. There was also the issue that many of them were teenagers who openly consumed alcohol in broad daylight. We had to draw the line somewhere."

Greg was stunned. It was shocking enough that Officer Bob agreed to an interview with Tommy, but Greg never would have guessed in a million years he'd have nice things to say about the punk scene back then.

Stanley was only a couple of years into his career in those days, beginning his climb through the ranks. But he knew many of the local teens because of his involvement as a coach in the local little league. The Salem brothers stand out in his memory to this day. "The older brother, Tim, was really quiet. Mostly kept to himself until he got a few drinks in him. Then he'd unleash that sarcastic humor of his on anybody who was around. The younger brother, Greg, didn't need booze to get worked up. That kid was always looking for a fight."

BCC, as they are more commonly known, started out as a passion project for Tim the summer before his junior year in high school. He'd gotten a guitar for his thirteenth birthday, but didn't play it in public for a couple of years. By then he had developed an aggressive strumming style that would become a signature feature of the band's earliest songs. "Dude turned into a total shredder overnight. I had no idea he played guitar until he showed up with it at school one day and said he was starting a band with his little bro," said BCC drummer, Marco Johnson.

Greg slammed the book down onto the desk. It was one thing for Officer Bob to give an interview without letting him know, but Marco? They practically lived together for the last six months, ever since Greg saved his life. The least he would expect is a heads up that his drummer was spewing quotes about Greg and his brother. He decided to say something about it to Marco right then.

Greg felt the blood rushing up into his face as he pounded across the backyard for the house. He went inside intending to call his drummer, but spotted his car keys first. Yelling at Marco in person suddenly seemed like a much better idea.

He snatched his phone and keys, stepping back out onto the deck. He was half way across the yard when two men stepped out from the shadows on either side of him. Both were wearing baggy black suits and had identical slicked-back hair. They advanced on him without saying a word.

Greg pivoted, ducking down to deliver a solid uppercut to the goon on his left. He spun around for the guy on his right when the points of a crackling Taser connected with the soft skin on his neck. Greg could smell his own flesh burning; his knees buckled and he hit the ground. He listened to his son crying somewhere inside the house as one of the men slipped a black bag over his head.

They handcuffed his wrists and stood him up before hauling him through the back gate. The tips of his sneakers dragged on the ground behind him as they rushed him to their car. Greg felt like he might be sick. He'd been on rides like this before. They never ended well.

Chapter 6

The trip was mercifully short and painless, aside from the handcuffs digging into his wrists. They let Greg ride in the backseat, instead of the trunk, which he took as a good sign. He'd driven those winding cliff roads enough to have a good idea where they were headed, despite the bag over his head. It wasn't much of a surprise when they pulled him from the backseat and shoved him up the marble steps of the Flores Estate.

It took a moment for his eyes to adjust to the light when they pulled the bag from his head. The entryway alone was bigger than Greg's entire property in South Bay. They pushed him along a hallway and into a high-ceilinged living room. Everything was painted a stark white that glowed against the dark, wooden floors. Several enormous paintings lined the walls, each splattered with a different color of neon paint. Bass-heavy, electronic dance music thumped from the tiny, surround-sound speakers mounted at careful angles high up near the intricate crown molding. It might have been a modern art museum if it weren't for the stodgy antique furniture in the center of the room.

They led Greg to a purple velvet sofa, forcing him to sit. The two men walked out of the room in stride. Neither of them had said a single word since the moment they snatched Greg from his backyard. He was impressed with their no-nonsense approach to getting shit done, but hoped he'd never see either of them again—at least not alive.

Left to his own devices, Greg stood up and began inspecting the room. An oil painting hung over the garage-sized fireplace, featuring a naked Gabriella lying on her stomach. It felt like her eyes followed him over to the large picture window looking into the backyard. There was an Olympic-sized pool out there, lined on one side with the type of canvas cabanas you'd find at a Vegas resort. A squat pool house sat beyond that, with floor-to-ceiling windows tinted the color of black smoke.

Turning around, he found a bookcase built into the opposite wall on the far side of the room. Throne-shaped chairs were arranged around an egg-shaped coffee table. A small man sat there with his elbows on the curving arms, legs crossed before him. His fingers formed a steeple under a pointed chin, while his dark eyes bored into Greg's.

"Did you screw my wife?"

It sounded soft and effeminate. The kind of voice that should have been accompanied by a lisp, but this man's words were as short and sharp as his features. Each one delivered with a precision suggesting he had all the time in the world, but none to waste.

Greg folded his arms, furrowing his brow.

"It's a good question, but I'm afraid you'll have to be more specific."

The man sighed. He stood up to remove his sport coat, carefully laying it across the chair. Next, he rolled the sleeves of his designer dress shirt until they were up near his bony elbows. He cracked his neck with the palms of his hands and sauntered toward Greg. His hair went from a soft brown color to dark black the closer he got.

He didn't stop until his chest was only a few inches from Greg's.

"The tabloids seem to think you did. Which would be a problem since I hired you and your little friend to keep her from whoring around."

Greg thought his eyes were playing tricks on him. The man, who had looked so slight across the room, was only a few inches shorter than him up close.

"That's not the way I heard it. We thought you wanted us to take some pictures. Give you proof."

"You haven't answered my question."

"And you still haven't introduced yourself. It's the least you could do after having your bodyguards drag me out of my home."

"Name's Tony Flores. Now tell me. I know you wanted to, everybody else does. It kind of turns me on."

Flores hissed those last few words. Greg instinctively took a step back, to keep himself from throwing a punch. Things were getting weird a little too fast.

"Sorry to disappoint you. Where is she now?"

"I hoped *you* might know."

Flores raised an eyebrow before Greg could go on.

"She stayed in my guest house. I was in bed with my wife."

Flores tightened his lips, bobbing his head in a spastic fit of laughter. Greg couldn't figure out if he was coming unhinged or getting ready to pull a gun. Several uncomfortable seconds passed before Flores gathered himself enough to speak again.

"You're a better man than I am. I had her bent over the mixing board in my studio on the first night of our recording session. Cost me a fortune in alimony with the ex, but I have to say it was worth every penny. Take a seat."

Greg walked backward slowly, never taking his eyes off of Flores. He sat down on the sofa again, while Flores took the lounge chair opposite him.

"Is it true? Gabriella told me you and your partner saved her at the golf club."

Greg nodded. It was the most he could manage while trying to figure out this twisted relationship. Flores was easily thirty years older than Gabriella, and a total scumbag to boot. A music industry dinosaur that probably made a mint exploiting young artists who mistook his fake praise and free coke as a sign they'd made it. And then, when he drew the unsuspecting newbies far enough into his web, he'd put a contract in front of them giving him all the rights to their music forever. A lot of them had signed, by the looks of the place. *Every musician in Hollywood gets bent over a mixing board at some point.*

Flores smiled as if confirming Greg's assessment of him.

"I know what you're thinking. 'What's an old geezer like this doing with a hot piece of ass like her?' The answer's obvious—I've got money and the keys to her future. But I really do love her, despite the nature of our relationship. Which is why I'm thankful to you and Mateo for saving her from those guys at the country club."

Greg thought about correcting him, deciding it was better that he didn't know Marco's real name.

"You have a funny way of showing it. Weren't you worried the paparazzi would see your goons drag me in?"

"They aren't out there all the time; only when somebody big does a recording session here. Besides, my men brought you in through the delivery gate around back."

"Convenient. Guess you're not worried the hired help will rat you out."

"Don't be fooled by the big house. I don't keep a full-time staff here. That's an old-fashioned waste of money."

Greg wanted to ask him why the ugly neon paintings didn't fall into the same category, but bit his tongue instead.

"Well, you didn't have to kidnap me if you only wanted to talk."

The expression on Flores' face changed in an instant, from open and friendly to blank. He was either high as a kite, or damaged from decades in the fast lane.

"You got off easy compared to what I have in mind for the douche bags who tried to hurt her."

Greg could only imagine what those two frat boys would endure at the hands of Tony and his men. Then again, they'd probably get what they deserve if he believed Gabriella's version of what happened. He was going over the events in the hotel room again when Tony interrupted his thoughts.

"I told you I love her, and love can make a man jealous. So I had to know if you banged her or I wouldn't feel comfortable thanking you. But that's not the only reason you're here. I have a business proposition for you."

"Thanks, but we're actually leaving town for a couple of weeks. So, I'm not really looking for any extra work right now."

Flores smiled, renewed light behind his eyes.

"Not many people realize it these days, but I got my start producing rock bands. I want to get back into it again, but haven't come across the right opportunity. Until I heard that you were getting Bad Citizen Corporation back together."

Greg was speechless. Flores didn't seem to notice.

"Let me show you my studio."

They wound their way out of the house and across the backyard, skirting the pool the whole way. Flores slid the pool house door open to reveal a state-of-the-art recording studio hidden inside. Gold and platinum records lined the soundproofed walls along with an endless collection of vintage guitars. The large recording room was completely set up for a session—amplifiers, drums, keyboards, and microphone stands—but the chairs in the adjacent mixing room were empty.

Flores took a seat behind the board, immediately tweaking knobs. Greg found it hard not to imagine Gabriella in there on that first night described to him in such vivid detail. He wanted to leave as soon as possible, but knew he'd have to suffer through some contemporary pop music first.

Rhythmic breathing was the first thing Greg heard when Flores brought the faders up. A heavy kick drumbeat came in next, accented with erratic flourishes of cymbals and snare. Thunderous, chugging bass notes brought the energy up a few notches, moments before a woman unleashed a string of rapid-fire words delivered almost too fast for Greg to understand. He didn't recognize Gabriella's voice until the song reached the chorus and the rapper started singing.

Flores saw the look on his guest's face and quickly brought the volume down.

"Pretty incredible, right?"

"Stunning. Where'd you find her?"

"Saw her at a club downtown, doing a collaboration with another street rapper named Big J. They used to run with the same gang in high school or something. I tracked her down backstage after the show and the rest, as they say, is history."

"You have a good ear. When's this record coming out?"

"Already did, last year. Biggest commercial flop of my career."

༄

GREG SUFFERED THROUGH ANOTHER hour before Flores finally let him go. They'd listened to some of his more successful singles, and even got into a few of the early rock acts he'd worked with—every one of them an eighties hair-metal band. Greg had to admit it was a pretty impressive body of work, but not exactly the sound he was looking for with the next BCC record. It didn't keep him from making promises that would get him out of there.

The last thing Flores said still bounced around Greg's mind as the bodyguards drove him home.

"You can't just put a record out and pretend like you're still twenty years old. That'll look pathetic. I can help you make something *now*, something relevant."

Despite the seeds of doubt planted by Flores, the ride home was a lot like the ride there—minus the bag and handcuffs. They rode in silence the whole way. The radio wasn't even turned on, which left Greg to look out at the moonlight reflecting off the ocean. He was happy to be going home in one piece, but didn't look forward to his unresolved fight with Kristen. Or letting Marco have it for sleeping with Gabriella and almost getting him killed. His feelings of rage were only amplified when he remembered the interview his drummer did for *Among the Grizzlies*.

It was late when they finally dropped him off in the alley behind his house. Greg jumped out, slamming the door without looking back. He stepped around the El Camino, pushed the gate open, and headed into the garage. Everything was right where he'd left it, including his thoughts. He slumped down into a chair and picked up Tommy's book. He wanted to read Marco's passage again, to see if he'd overreacted earlier.

It took moment to realize he'd flipped to the wrong chapter. This one had an unfortunately familiar title—"I Am Tim." He scanned the page with angry eyes, quickly landing on a passage somewhere in the middle:

"Dude killed himself, simple as that. Seems like a million years ago, but the biggest bummer is that we'll probably never know why. I think that's what pisses Greg off the most," Johnson said.

Greg flung the book across the room, watching with satisfaction as it shattered a picture frame on the opposite wall. He stood up, checking to make sure the keys were still in his pocket. The El Camino was waiting for him out back, like always. For the moment, it seemed like that car was the only thing in his life he could trust. He climbed in, punching the steering wheel before rumbling off.

Greg sped along Bay Cities Boulevard. Black Flag tore through "Police Van" on the stereo as he stepped on the gas to blow through a yellow light. He was heading to Marco's to kick his ass for giving Tommy the interview, but he also wanted to know if Gabriella was there. If she was, that ass kicking might turn into murder.

Greg got within a few blocks of Marco's condo, but pulled into the parking lot at Eddie's instead. He wanted to see if JJ was working before he dropped in on Marco unannounced. Things would be a lot easier if his roommate wasn't around to get involved, especially since he was also a member of the band. Not that it would stop Greg the way he felt at the moment.

Greg threw the car into park, climbed out, and walked over to the entrance of Eddie's. He stuck his head inside, finding the place empty except for a couple of regulars drunkenly talking at the bar. Pennywise played in the background as the bartender, another new face he didn't recognize, closed out a tab at the register. Greg's eyes shifted to all the liquor bottles lit up on the mirrored shelf behind the bar. His mouth began to water.

He spun around in retreat, instinctively heading for Junior's house on foot. He knew she'd be asleep, but he needed some fresh air and a little distance from the bar. It was as if a switch had been flipped. All of the anger and betrayal Greg felt funneled into an unquenchable thirst for oblivion. Each step on the cracked sidewalk became an internal battle. Right foot—*Just one drink.* Left foot—*Don't do it.*

His decision was made before he even reached the next corner. The liquor store where he'd wasted so many afternoons playing video games with his brother as a kid was still open. The blinding lights were like a beacon, a wink and a nod from the universe.

Greg jogged across the boulevard. It had been years since he stepped inside, so he doubted they would recognize him. He went over to the cooler and grabbed a six-pack of beer before heading to the counter. The old man rang him up without any hesitation. Empowered, Greg decided to push his luck.

"And a fifth of Vodka, too."

Chapter 7

*T*he kid in the blue hat had his hands around Greg's throat. He dug his fingernails into the skin, tearing at the rope burns already there. Greg tried to fight back, but had no control over his arms. They flopped limp at his sides as the flow of air got cut off from his lungs. His head felt like an expanding balloon already well past the breaking point. The kid's eyes were dead, but his lips were moving, repeating the same six words again and again—"If you wanna die with me... If you wanna die with me... If you wanna die with me... If you wanna die with me..."

Greg sprang up in a panic. A record spun on the turntable, skipping over and over on the same scratch. It was "If You Wanna," the last track on side one of Bad Citizen Corporation's first album. He reached down from the couch, groping the floor for his phone to check the time. His hand came back with the bottle of vodka instead. He twisted the cap to take a big gulp, hurling it at the stereo once it was empty. The needle scratched across the vinyl with a loud shriek before the arm snapped off. The record spun to a stop as Greg stood up.

He found the phone in the pocket of his jeans. It was close to seven, the latest he'd slept in weeks. Greg noticed three missed calls from Marco, two from last night and one from this morning. He hit the "Call Back" button and waited for an answer, his fury amplified by a staggering hangover.

"Dude, where the hell have you been?"

"Stayed up late reading a book. It's called *Among*—""

Greg became aware of his own tattered voice, but Marco didn't seem to notice.

"Whatever. You have to get up to Gabriella's place. Like, right now."

Greg cleared his throat to no avail.

"What's going on? Please tell me you didn't do anything stupid. *Again.*"

"Matter of opinion, bro. Get over here as soon as you can. And bring your gun."

Marco hung up. Greg stared at his phone for a second, deciding what to do. He guessed Kristen would freak out that he never came to bed, but there weren't any missed calls from her. And there was no way he could face her in his current condition. He needed time to get his head—and his story—straight. The pursuit of marital bliss would have to wait.

He stumbled to the bathroom for a quick shower.

✎

GREG WAS RELIEVED HE kept clean clothes and a toothbrush in the office. He still looked bloated and pale, but at least he didn't smell like the storeroom at Eddie's any longer. If anybody could tell he'd fallen off the wagon, it was Marco. He knew his partner wouldn't tell Kristen or anybody else, but it might set a bad precedent for the BCC tour. Greg falling off the wagon paled in comparison to what a Marco relapse would look like. All bets were off if they both started drinking again at the same time.

Forty-five minutes passed before Greg pulled the El Camino along the curb behind Marco's ride. They were a couple hundred yards down the block from the front gates of the Flores Estate. Marco spotted Greg right away in the rearview mirror, waving him over to the passenger seat of his car.

Greg popped a mint and slid across to his passenger door. He climbed out, staying low as he crept to Marco's car. The door swung open to greet him.

"Hurry up. Get in."

Greg did as he was told, softly shutting the door behind him.

"What the hell is going on, Marco? Please tell me you haven't been up here all night."

Greg already knew the answer, judging by the mingled smells of body odor and stale coffee. Marco didn't seem to notice or care that he reeked. His eyes spun like pinwheels as he spoke.

"Some shit went down last night."

"For your information, we aren't on this case anymore."

"She came to my place, okay?"

Greg slapped the dashboard in response.

"Jesus, dude. Calm down. I drove her home around three in the morning."

"After you slept with her again?"

"So what if it did?"

"I met her husband last night. His name's Tony Flores and he's a bit of head case. Two of his men dragged me up here while you were getting your rocks off."

Marco shook his head.

"Didn't go down like that, bro. She cried on my shoulder for a couple of hours about how scared she was. Then I drove her home. End of story."

"Then what the hell are we doing up here?"

"I told her to flash the lights in one of the upstairs windows when she got in bed. It never happened, so I waited."

"Are you in high school or something? She probably forgot and fell asleep. Or maybe she decided to screw her husband. These people are seriously weird."

"Maybe so, but I stuck around just in case. Then, right before I called you the last time, I thought I heard something. Loud popping sounds."

Greg craned to look out the back window of the car.

"I don't see any cops. Neighborhood like this, somebody would definitely call nine-one-one if they heard gunshots."

"They came from deep inside the house. The nearest neighbor is half a mile away, at least."

Greg shook his head in disgust.

"Sounds like you've got it all figured out. Tell me why I'm here."

"We need to make sure she's safe."

"Call her."

Marco rolled his eyes.

"Give me a fucking break. She hasn't picked up or responded to my texts since she went inside."

Greg groaned, disappointed to see his partner so blinded by love.

"Because she's asleep."

"Or on the ground bleeding."

"You've got a good imagination."

"That's what you said when we saved Gabriella at the The Cliffs."

It was a low blow, but Greg had it coming. Marco swung his door open to get out. Greg took a deep breath and followed right behind his partner, gun in hand. Soon they were standing in front of the locked front gates.

Marco wove his hands together to lift Greg over the fence. He waited until his partner touched down on the other side before scaling the bars himself. That seemed to be where his plan ended.

"What now, bro?"

"Let's go around back. We can try the door by the pool."

They followed a stone path winding through an impressive garden. Greg stopped to check the ground floor windows every few yards, but didn't see any movement inside. They soon reached the back patio, finding the pool and cabanas empty like the day before. Greg motioned Marco over to the back door.

"We can get into the house right there, but let's check the studio first. I think that's where Flores spends most of his time."

They edged around the pool, checking to make sure the coast was clear with every step. Greg listened carefully for any music coming from inside of the pool house, but heard nothing. He slid the door open with the tip of his shoe, motioning for Marco to stand behind him.

Greg stepped inside with his gun out in front of him to clear the room. Everything looked exactly the same as the last time he'd been there. He led Marco over to the mixing room. They saw the body as soon as they walked through the door. Tony Flores was slumped over the board, the right side of his head spread out across the dials and knobs. Fresh drops of blood fell from the edge, splashing to the wooden floor like gruesome little waterfalls.

Marco backed out of the room, his eyes on the corpse. Greg crouched down to inspect the ground for a gun.

"This wasn't a suicide."

Marco bolted from the studio, sprinting to the main house. Greg barely had time to react before his friend was gone.

"Don't touch anything!"

Marco barreled through the backdoor and into the living room, Greg right behind him. One of the two bodyguards that snatched him was lying at Marco's feet. Red blossoms of blood spread out across his white dress shirt, soaking the lapels of his coat. He saw the second bodyguard slumped in one of the chairs near the bookshelves across the room. Greg made sure he wasn't breathing before returning to his partner's side. Marco looked up at the painting of Gabriella with tears in his eyes.

"We have to find her."

"One way or another, we will."

Greg pulled a gun from the closest bodyguard's shoulder holster, shoving it into Marco's shaking hand. His wrist went limp under the weight. It looked like the weapon might fall to the floor.

"Don't drop it. It might go off."

Marco's face went green before fading to a ghostly white.

"No way, bro."

"You don't have a choice. We have to search the rest of the house, but the killer might still be here."

Marco nodded in agreement, his tense body telegraphing a different response. Greg knew they had to get this over with fast. It was only a matter of time before the cops showed up or the killers popped up. He prayed it wasn't Gabriella, but couldn't rule out the possibility.

They went door to door downstairs, searching every room. Neither of them had been upstairs before, so that took a little longer. In the end, they didn't find anything or anybody else to tell them what happened. Gabriella might still be missing, but they needed to get out of there. Greg took the gun from Marco's hand and wiped it down before putting it back in the dead bodyguard's holster. He did the same with the knob on the back door while Marco watched him work.

"We have to call the cops, bro."

"No shit, but they don't have to know we searched the place. I'll call it in from the car."

ை

THEY WERE BACK AT Greg's house before Marco finally spoke again. His question caught Greg off guard.

"When did you start boozing again?"

Greg had almost forgotten himself, given everything that happened since last night. They pulled up behind the garage and Greg killed the engine. The El Camino sputtered and shook before she went still.

"I'm not 'boozing again.' I screwed up last night, but it's not a permanent situation."

"It better not be, bro. I'm looking at you to keep *my* ass sober when we're on tour. Not so sure I can pull it off on my own."

"Don't worry. Everything will be fine. But while we're on the subject—when were you going to tell me about the interview you did with Tommy?"

"Huh? Dude interviewed everybody in town. I'm guessing that's one book you'll want to skip, unless you like being pissed off all the time."

Greg couldn't argue with his logic, and he was too wiped out to try. Marco was first through the back gate, immediately heading for the garage. Greg stopped him before he could open the door.

"You don't want to go in there. I still need to clean...after last night."

"Just like the good old days."

They ambled into the house together instead. Marco took a seat at the kitchen table while Greg went into the bedroom to find Kristen. He came back out holding an envelope and a folded piece of paper.

Marco took one look at his face and knew something was wrong.

"What's up?"

"She's gone. Kristen took the baby and left. They're staying with Junior."

"Looks like we're heading back over to North Bay."

"Not right now."

"You sure, bro?"

Marco's skepticism only made Greg's worse. In the end, he decided not to play the hero this time around. If Kristen wanted to talk, she knew where to find him.

"I need to give her space. Sometimes you have to let people go when they've made up their mind. Besides, we still need to call those murders in."

"And clean the fucking office up. You have interviews to do."

October 1998—10:00 p.m.

Tim slowly brought his head up from the desk. A thick string of saliva momentarily kept him anchored to the puddle he'd left behind. Prince Buster worked his way through "Al Capone" on the stereo in the background.

It was hard to say how long he'd been nodding out, but somebody else was in the office with him now. He opened his eyes, the kaleidoscopic images dancing around each other for a moment before snapping into the solid form of Junior. She had a black leather jacket on over a torn Adolescents "I Hate Children" T-shirt and red bondage pants. Her head was shaved short except for a small fringe of blue bangs hanging over furious eyes.

"Wake up, you fucking junkie."

Tim groaned and sat back, the chair creaking beneath him. His blood flowed again, giving a second life to his last hit. He could feel himself retreating back into the dark corners of his mind, blissfully aware he was hiding out in the open.

Junior's voice drew closer—more full of disgust—the next time he heard it.

"I said, get up!"

She slapped his face for emphasis. Tim jumped up, kicking the chair behind him.

"What the fuck?!"

His eyes adjusted to the room, as if seeing Junior for the first time.

"Oh, hey. I like your hair."

"Gee, thanks. It hasn't changed much in the last few minutes."

Tim rubbed his face, collecting his thoughts. His eyes darted to the clock on the wall. Junior read his panic correctly.

"Don't worry, I locked up for you." She slammed the cash box down onto the desk. It sounded precisely as pathetic and empty as it was. "You're lucky I came in here tonight. One of your other customers might have gone on a shopping spree. They could've wiped you out."

"Uh, thanks. Have you seen my cigarettes?"

Tim stumbled into the desk. He made a show of groping the papers scattered there, searching frantically for a balloon and syringe. Junior grabbed his wrist, yanking him back into a standing position.

"I know what you're looking for and I know where it is."

Tim managed a disarming smile. He'd use those teeth to bite her throat if she didn't give his dope back.

"Where is it?"

"I need some answers first. Have you seen Marco tonight?"

"What? Yeah, he was in here earlier. Hitting me up for money, like usual."

"Big surprise. Did you give him anything?"

"Twenty, I think. He wants me to get BCC back together. Why do *you* care?"

"I think the little fucker broke into my car. He took my purse and wallet."

"Come on, Junior. Marco wouldn't do that to you."

They both knew it was bullshit, but Junior had less of a problem admitting it.

"Ha! You losers would hock my organs for dope. Where'd he go?"

"Said he had to meet somebody at that motel by the freeway."

"Damn it! I just came from there. He's already gone."

Tim dragged his chair over, slumping down into it. Junior took the seat across from him, slamming his stash down on the desk. She was impressed he managed to wait a beat before lunging.

"Don't shoot that shit in front of me."

Tim made a beeline for the bathroom. She heard him going through his ritual in there—biting at the balloon full of heroin, cooking it in the black-bottomed spoon, drawing it up with the syringe's plunger.

The man who emerged a few minutes later looked slightly more human than the desperate junkie who'd left. Junior knew it was only a temporary improvement.

She stood up to leave.

"Take care of yourself, Tim."

"Whoa. Where are you going?"

"As fun as it sounds to sit around and watch you nod off, I think I'll go cancel my credit cards instead. I'm glad you're feeling better, though."

"I only did a little for maintenance. Hang out for a few. I've got wine here somewhere."

Tim went to the filing cabinet, pulling out a half-full bottle and a red plastic cup. He twisted the lid and poured her a drink. She gave it a quick sniff before taking a sip.

"Would you ever consider it?"

Tim scratched his head, wondering how he'd managed to miss a whole conversation again.

"Huh?"

"Getting BCC back together."

"Oh…"

"No big deal. I was being selfish. I mean you guys are my favorite band."

"Thanks, but it's not really up to me. Your boyfriend's calling the shots now."

"Who, Greg? We broke up like a month ago." She forced a laugh pregnant with self-doubt. "Where the hell have you been?"

Tim nodded to the syringe on the desk, raising an eyebrow.

"Time flies when you're fucked up all the time."

She finished her wine, reaching over to pour a refill. Tim watched her, wondering if his brother's biggest mistake was breaking up the band or breaking up with Junior.

She caught him looking, but didn't let on.

"Why are you trying to kill yourself? I mean, I get it, you're like a punk rock god around The Bay Cities, but you don't have to die to prove how cool you are."

"'Punk rock god' is a little strong."

"We all looked up to you, that's all."

"Seems like Greg's the one that everybody worships these days. Do you think I held him back? You know, by making him play the music I like instead of what he's into."

"It's not one or the other. You guys are great together. That's why it sucks so much to watch you imploding, or whatever you think you're doing. But if you're asking me if Greg should keep playing music, even if you don't want to—the answer's yes."

She downed the rest of her refill and stood. Tim watched her from his chair, trying to imagine a universe where they might have ended up together. He wondered if there really were alternate realities waiting for him out there; other places where he might have the chance to be a better person.

She walked around the desk, bending over to give him a peck on the cheek.

"I mean it, Tim. Take care of yourself."

He grabbed her by the shirt, pulling her in for a real kiss. Their lips met and for a brief moment he could taste a different reality. Tim believed he might have finally found a reason to wake up tomorrow morning. It was over fast.

She reared back, punching him hard on the cheek. The physical pain didn't hold a candle to watching his happy fantasy crumble to the floor.

"What the fuck is wrong with you?! I told you that could never happen again."

"I just...you said that you and Greg aren't—"

She stood up, her chest heaving with rage.

"Jesus, Tim. He's still your brother. Is this how you're planning to get back at him for breaking up the band? By screwing his ex-girlfriend again?"

Tim shook his head, shame filling the entire room.

"He's not breaking up the band. He wants to keep playing without me. Without any of us."

Chapter 8

The set-up was simple enough. Greg had a conference line he dialed into every thirty minutes for the next six hours. The press blitz was all in support of the BCC tour that started tomorrow. It included conversations with writers from a variety of music publications. Marco had already promised to keep the coffee flowing all day, and even offered to buy lunch. Lindsay, one of the two Dead March PR reps Greg met at Eddie's, would also be on the line listening in "just in case." Greg couldn't decide if she was there for his protection or the journalists', but knew they'd find out soon enough.

It was shaping up to be a pretty busy day. Greg was pleased when he managed to stay sober the previous night. Talking about himself all day was miserable enough, but doing it with a hangover would be unbearable. It had been a lot easier with Marco refusing to leave his side, although he would never admit it. In addition to the back-to-back interviews, Greg and Marco also had to stop by the BCPD to give their official statements about what they'd seen at the Flores Estate. From there they were supposed to meet the rest of the band at the rehearsal space to do a last-minute run-through of the set, then pack the van. They would also be meeting the tour manager for the first time.

With everything else going on, Greg worried he might not see his wife or son before taking off for two weeks. He swore to himself that he'd make time to say goodbye before he picked up the phone to dial in for his first interview.

"This is Greg."

"Hey, Greg. This is Lindsay. You ready for the big day?"

"Ready as I'll ever be."

"You'll do great. Stay relaxed, and have fun. It'll be all softball questions today, but I'll jump in if I hear anything that's out of line. Otherwise, be yourself and don't be afraid to be a little *shocking*."

Greg didn't get the chance to ask what she meant. Then another voice joined the conversation. It was a young woman with a British accent.

"Hi! This is Sandra Lowney with *Music News International*. Is that Greg?"

"It is. How's it going?"

"Good. I know we only have fifteen minutes, so I'll jump right in. Tell me how you met Gabriella Flores."

"Gabriella? I'm sorry, I thought we were talking about—"

"Is it true that you two are an item?"

Greg wanted to stop the interview by describing the bodies he and Marco found the night before, but didn't think it would go over well. And since Lindsay hadn't jumped in, he decided it was best to play along.

"You shouldn't believe everything you read."

"I was actually referring to the pictures. But since you don't seem interested in answering—"

"We're definitely *not* an item."

"Well, that makes more sense. I mean, given the age difference."

Greg wanted to point out that Gabriella's current—late—husband was even older, but guessed it would come back to bite him in the ass once word got out about the murders. Especially if people found out Marco actually slept with her. He tried to change the topic instead.

"You sound pretty young yourself. Why the interest in an old hardcore band like Bad Citizen Corporation?"

"I, um, actually had this story assigned. But I did listen to some of your music. It's very *loud*."

A clicking sound interrupted them and, just like that, Lindsay was back on the line.

"All right. That's all the time we had scheduled for you two. If you need any more info, don't hesitate to reach out to me directly. I'll be happy to get you whatever you need."

The reporter thanked them both before hanging up. Greg wanted to do the same, but Lindsay stopped him.

"Sorry about that. I had no idea she was only interested in the gossipy stuff. You handled yourself pretty well. The next one's scheduled in fifteen—sorry, thirteen minutes. Talk soon."

Marco waited for Greg at the kitchen table with a fresh mug of coffee. He had a laptop open, doing research of some kind.

"How'd it go out there?"

"Terrible. She asked a lot about Gabriella. Have you heard from her, by the way?"

"Not yet. I've called and texted a few times, but got nothing."

Greg could see the concern etched into his friend's face. He did his best to calm him down, even though he didn't like lying.

"I'm sure she's fine, Marco. She's really tough. She'll turn up."

"Thanks, bro. I'm hoping she left a message for me at my pad."

"Why don't you go home and check. I can handle things here. Have you called JJ?"

"A couple of times. He's been out all morning getting ready for the tour, but he said he hasn't heard anything either."

"Go home and get packed. I'll meet you back here later on."

Marco slammed the laptop shut, leaving through the front door. Greg went back out to the garage for his second phone interview.

"This is Greg."

"Hey, man. It's Patrick from *CoreNoMore* magazine, a hardcore zine out of Vancouver. We did an interview a few years ago."

Greg's shoulder's instantly relaxed. At least he would have one normal conversation today, talking about the only thing that really mattered—the music.

"I remember, and I have to tell you, I'm thrilled to hear your voice."

"Thanks, man. Stoked you guys are going back out on the road. How long do we have to wait before you get up to Canada?"

"Not too long, I hope. What did you want to know today?"

"Actually, if you don't mind, I really want to talk about your brother, Tim."

"Okay…"

"I just finished that book, *Among the Grizzlies*. All the parts about his suicide blew me away. Have you read it?"

"Not all of it. No."

"That author really makes him out to be some kind of punk rock hero. Like he died so that Bad Citizen Corporation could become legendary. You have any thoughts about that?"

"Only that it sounds ridiculous. Tim wasn't some martyr with a grand plan. He was a junkie with the weight of the world on his shoulders. A weight that he put there himself."

"I'm glad you brought that up. Last time we spoke, you said your brother's death wasn't a suicide, but now it seems like maybe you've changed your mind."

"I haven't changed my mind about anything…except maybe this interview."

Greg heard Lindsay apologizing on the line when he killed the call. He pushed the chair back with his foot, slamming the garage door as he headed for the house. Marco was gone, but somebody else waited for him at the kitchen table when he walked in. It looked like she and their son had both been crying all night.

"I'm so glad you came back. I was really worried about you."

She sniffled while patting their son. He clung to her arms, half asleep and mindlessly playing with his pacifier.

"You have a funny way of showing it. You didn't even call."

"I wanted to give you space. Look, I know things have been crazy around here lately. It's not fair to you or Timmy."

Kristen strained at him, studying his face. She didn't seem pleased with what she saw there.

"You stayed out all night again."

"Sorry about that. We got caught up on a job."

"With that woman?"

"Gabriella? Yes, but no. It's her husband and a few of his men. We, uh, found them dead at their house."

This seemed to get her attention.

"What about that woman?"

"We don't know where she is. Marco's actually out looking for her right now, but that's for the police to figure out."

"I'm glad to hear you say that. I just wish you weren't leaving us."

She reached a hand out across the table. Greg took it, looking his wife in the eyes for the first time in too many weeks.

"It's only a couple of weeks. I'll be making a record for a few months when we get back. We'll be able to spend plenty of time together then. I promise."

Tears rolled down Kristen's cheeks. The baby, however, was mercifully asleep. It seemed like the first chance they'd had to speak like adults in months.

"It's going to be okay, Kristen."

"Is it? It doesn't seem like you want anything to do with us."

She looked down at the baby in her arms, slipping a pinky into his little fist. Greg knew she was right, that he'd been pulling away. But this wasn't the time to discuss their future. He wanted to wait it out, hoping everything would get back to some version of normal once the tour ended.

"I love you both more than anything. Things are moving too fast right now."

She let out a soft sob, bringing a hand up to her face.

"I can't be the girl that you rescued from the mountains for the rest of my life. I'm a mom now, and your wife. I thought that's what you wanted."

"It was—I mean, it is. I just wish we had more time before starting a family."

"I wanted that, too, Greg, but I wouldn't change a thing if it meant not having Timmy. This is the first time in my life I've had a normal family and it feels like it's already slipping away from me."

"It's not. I won't let it." Greg's phone started dinging in his pocket. He stood up to fish it out, looking at the text messages waiting there.

"Oh crap! I have to go do an interview. Wait here for me here. Promise you won't leave again."

"I promise."

ॐ

"THIS IS GREG."

"Hey, man. It's Tommy."

Greg caught his breath. Nothing about this day was going according to plan.

"Lindsay, is this for real?"

Greg waited for the PR rep to chime in, but got no response. Tommy read the situation, trying to help Greg make sense of the chaos.

"Sorry. This magazine I'm writing for thought it would be a good idea to have me do a surprise interview with you. You know, reunite the two guys whose lives were changed by my book. I thought it would be funny...until now..."

"It's fine. I wasn't expecting to hear your voice, is all."

Tommy laughed, clearly annoyed.

"Good thing or a bad thing?"

"Not what I expected. That's all. Things are kind of hectic now."

"Tell me about it. I haven't been home in almost a month thanks to this never-ending book tour. You getting excited for the BCC shows?"

"It's hard to know how to feel. So much has happened in the last few years."

Tommy went quiet for a moment, chewing on everything Greg said.

"People are always telling me how much they love the parts of the book that you're in."

Greg couldn't hold his frustration back any longer.

"When were you going to tell me that you interviewed my friends?"

"Was I supposed to get your permission first or something?"

"It would have been the right thing to do, since this is my story."

The words felt odd leaving Greg's mouth. Like he'd exposed himself to the world. Tommy must have sensed it, too. He pounced.

"*Your* story? You might have been at the center of all this crazy shit, but it effected everybody around you. You have no right to claim ownership."

"You named a chapter after my brother. He wasn't even there!"

"Jesus, Greg. He's with you everywhere you go. I tried writing about you without explaining Tim, but it didn't work. The story's the story."

"This book was supposed to be about Magnus and what happened up in the mountains. I didn't ask you to write my biography."

A sudden distance grew between them. It felt strange for their short, but intense friendship.

"Can I ask you something, Greg? Be honest with me."

"Shoot."

"Do you wish I'd never written *Among the Grizzlies*?"

Greg had no easy answer. He wasn't an outsider with a fresh perspective on Magnus Ursus, Bad Citizen Corporation, or Tim's death. Greg didn't come to these stories as somebody looking to be entertained, he'd lived through them—experienced every painful moment—and now they were in a bestseller written by somebody else; the collected headlines of Greg Salem's life, condensed down to a few chapters and spoon-fed to the world as a cautionary tale.

Greg was happy for Tommy and his success, but he still couldn't figure out exactly how he fit in. Except as a freak of nature that the world demanded to see in the flesh—for a little while, at least, until the next thing caught their attention. Greg wasn't sure if it would come as a relief or leave him wanting more.

A half-hearted "I don't know" was the most he could manage in response to Tommy's question.

Tommy had already hung up by the time Greg finally got the words out.

"Hey, Greg. It's Lindsay. Tommy texted me. Something came up and he had to cut the call short. He wanted me to apologize."

"Okay. I hope I didn't piss him off."

"I'm sure it's fine. Listen, I know you're busy today. I think we should cancel the rest of these interviews. That way you'll have more time to get ready for your tour."

Chapter 9

Greg was supposed to meet Marco at the BCPD station a few minutes before their appointment. Not much had changed since the last time he'd been there except for the unfamiliar faces coming and going through the glass doors out front. There was a time when he might have known some of them, bonded with them over their shared profession, but not anymore. He was on the other side of the law now, where you didn't need a badge to justify your gun.

Marco walked up at four o'clock on the dot. His thin blond hair was still wet from a shower, brushed back from his weathered face. Greg took one look at him and knew something was up.

"You're looking pretty beat up today."

"I'm worried about Gabriella. I mean, where the hell could she have gone? I watched her go in, but she never came out."

"That house is huge. There are plenty of ways she could have gotten out without you seeing her."

"She didn't have anything to do with those murders, bro."

"That's not what I meant, but what if she did? I know you think there's this magical bond between you because you slept with her, but that doesn't mean you know anything about her."

"Watch yourself. I'm not in the mood for this shit right now."

Greg grabbed him by the shoulders.

"It's just sex. She's probably slept with a few guys since then, too."

Marco shook free, stepping back. Greg could tell from the astonished look on his friend's face that he'd stepped over the line. He instantly regretted it.

"Sorry. Remember how we met her in the first place? She's trouble."

"Whatever, bro. You're gonna feel like a total dick when she comes back and proves you wrong."

Something about the confidence in Marco's voice set off alarms in Greg's head.

"Are you sure you don't know where she is?"

Marco was on the verge of giving an answer before Detective Bowers interrupted them. He had a cup of coffee in one hand and neatly folded newspaper tucked under his other arm.

"Let's go inside and get some answers about yesterday."

They followed him into the station. He waved them through at the front desk without slowing down, leading them down a familiar hallway. Greg wondered where Officer Bob was when they reached the door outside of his office. Detective Bowers cranked the knob to usher them inside.

The room was darker than usual, all of the natural light blocked out by closed blinds. Greg also noticed the desk had been moved to the opposite corner. None of the framed pictures on the wall looked familiar to him. Greg knew Officer Bob was retiring, but couldn't imagine it would happen this fast.

"When's your boss getting here?"

Detective Bowers ignored the question. He slapped the newspaper down on the desk and took a seat, motioning for his guests to do the same. They both remained standing.

"Suit yourselves, but we might be here a while."

Greg folded his arms, in a pathetic act of defiance.

"You mind telling us where Officer Bob is?"

"He's on medical leave. He asked me to give this to you. I told him it wasn't a good idea, but there you go."

He slid an envelope across the desk. Greg shoved it into his pocket without looking inside.

"Is he all right?"

"With Chief Stanley out, I'm in charge. Let's go over the events of last night."

Detective Bowers pulled a folder from the top drawer of his desk, flipping it open to reveal a stack of crime scene photos. The one on top was of Tony Flores, slumped on his mixing board with half of his head missing. Greg shifted his gaze, trying hard not to let the image get burned into his mind any more than it already was.

Detective Bowers turned to address Marco.

"Let's start with you. Care to tell me how you two made this discovery?"

Marco gave in and sat down. It looked like the weight of these killings had finally caught up with him.

"We were working a case for Flores. Keeping an eye on his wife."

"This her?"

He pushed a photo across the desk. It was a blurry snapshot of the painting from the living room at the Flores Estate. Marco couldn't stand to look at the image of Gabriella's naked body for too long.

"Yep."

"And you say that you were on assignment outside of the home where these murders took place?"

"Well, I mean—"

"Answer the question. Were you on assignment, or not?"

Greg put his hands down on the desk, reinserting himself into the conversation.

"He dropped her off at home before getting concerned about her safety."

Detective Bowers shifted his gaze from Marco's face to Greg's.

"So, he was there for personal reasons?"

His expression was all business, without any of the basic human compassion Greg had come to expect in this office. It was hard to fathom he might grow to miss Officer Bob.

"Yes, but don't jump to any conclusions. It started out as a—"

Detective Bowers brought a hand up, stopping Greg midsentence. He nodded to Marco instead, a look of pity on his face.

"Please tell me you aren't sleeping with her. If so, that brings you right to the top of the suspect list."

"I plead the fifth."

"This isn't a court."

Marco jumped up, pounding his fist on the desk.

"My point exactly. Those dudes got murdered and you're spending all your time trying to pin it on us. News flash, we didn't do it!"

Greg put his hand on Marco's chest, moving him back toward the door. Detective Bowers stood, jabbing a finger at them.

"Where do you two think you're going? I'm nowhere near finished with you yet."

Greg pushed Marco out into the hall. He muttered to himself when Greg shut the door. Detective Bowers came around the desk, sizing him up as he approached. He was pretty intimidating for his size, but Greg held his ground.

"You know damn well we didn't have anything to do with his."

"The only thing I know is that you and your friend have gotten used to making your own rules around here." Detective Bowers jabbed a thumb into his own chest. Greg did his best not to laugh. "That might have flown with the old Police Chief, but not the new one."

"So, it's official then?"

Detective Bowers jutted his chin out in a defiant scowl.

"Soon enough. I'm telling you right now, things will change pretty fast once it happens. Buckle up, buttercup."

"Meaning what?"

"No more special treatment for Greg Salem."

Greg shook his head in disbelief. He never had much faith in the BCPD, but at least Officer Bob understood the local community. He gave Detective Bowers and his police academy tough guy act a year at best.

"I'd be fine without the special treatment as long as I thought you could solve the occasional case without my help."

"Funny how you always seem to be at the center of things around here. Speaking of which, we closed the case on Tim Granger."

"Who?"

"That kid you found at the club."

"Oh, right. Let me guess…"

"We ruled it a copycat suicide, inspired by the death of your brother."

"Leave my brother out of this."

Detective Bowers winked.

"You probably have your friend Tommy's book to thank for that."

"What if you're wrong?"

"I'm not. Now sit down."

༄

THE REST OF THE band was already at the rehearsal space when Greg and Marco rolled up. Greg was still reeling from what Detective Bowers told him about the suicide, but there was no time to dwell on it. They still had a lot to get done before leaving on tour tomorrow. And Greg needed to get home at a reasonable hour so he could live up to his promise of spending some time with Kristen and their son.

Greg parked the El Camino among the usual sea of vans, converted airport shuttle busses, and sticker-covered hatchbacks. They walked over to join Chris and JJ near the entrance. Jerry was back behind the drum set, talking with somebody Greg didn't recognize. She was short and round, with sleeve tattoos and a constellation of piercings that traveled from her earlobes to her nose, eyebrows, and upper lip. Her hair was cut into a floppy pink Mohawk that looked like a toy horse's mane.

He slapped Chris on the back.

"That our new tour manager?"

"Not sure. She and Jerry were already there when we showed up."

JJ rolled his eyes and shrugged.

"Seems like they're old friends."

Greg wandered into the room, weaving his way through amplifiers and cymbal stands to reach them. The woman stood up when he arrived, extending a hand to shake. She might be tiny, but looked to be made of solid muscle.

"Tina Pierce. Dead March hired me to take care of you guys."

"Greg Salem."

"Oh, I know. I caught your show at Eddie's."

"You should have introduced yourself."

"You seemed pretty busy, and I had somewhere else to be later that night. I was telling The German here how great you guys were."

Greg looked over at Jerry. The guitar player gave a dismissive shrug, taking a long drag from his cigarette. Whatever he'd been chatting with Tina about, he didn't seem interested in continuing the conversation.

Greg turned back to his new tour manager, hoping she'd have more to say.

"'The German?'"

"Sorry. That's the nickname we gave him on a tour we did together last year. Right?"

Jerry grunted his assent before wandering off. Tina watched him go, a broad grin on her face.

"He's a great musician, but a major control freak when it comes to his gear. A few of the guys on the crew started calling him the 'Guitar Nazi.' I eventually convinced them to change it to 'The German' since we were mostly playing shows in The Fatherland at the time. No need to piss off the locals when you're a guest in their country. You know?"

Greg nodded. He liked her already, and not just because of the colorful info she had about their mysterious guitar player.

"What do you do when you aren't managing tours?"

"I'm an artist, actually. I mean, that's what I went to school for, although I don't have much time for it any more. It's mostly for fun these days."

"Cool. Are you a painter?"

"More like performance art, but enough about me. Let's meet the rest of the guys."

He led her over to where the band congregated, introducing her to Chris, JJ, and Marco in turn. She sized each of them up with a firm handshake.

"Ready to have some fun?"

She sounded like a little league team mom. Chris responded right away, the most animated he'd been in weeks.

"This is going to be so awesome."

"That's the spirit, Sparky. Now show me your gear so I can see what I've gotten myself into."

There it was. Chris already had a nickname before they'd even played their first show of the tour. Greg let her wander around the room cataloguing equipment with the rest of the band while he stepped outside for some fresh air. It was too early to know for sure, but something about her energy made it seem like things were finally coming together. He rolled the metal door down to give himself some space.

Greg was too deep in thought to notice the kid in the blue hat leaning against the El Camino's fender. He immediately broke into a sprint, inexplicably drawn to whatever roadblock the universe tried to throw at him now. The kid didn't budge, keeping his cool as Greg barreled toward him.

"What the hell are you doing here?"

"I've got my reasons. Surprised to see me?"

Greg clenched his fists, shifting from foot to foot. He wanted so badly to throw the first punch, but decided to take the high road. It's the least he could do considering everything he'd put this kid through. But he didn't have to be nice about it.

"Not really, since you've been following me around like some kind of stalker."

"I thought you saw me at the beach. I had a few things I wanted to say to you, but I couldn't find the right time."

"Until today."

The kid rolled his shoulders, working up to something big.

"Rumor has it you're leaving soon, so it's now or never."

"I'm all ears."

The kid stood. Greg leapt back, ready for a blow that never came.

"Chill out. I'm telling you, it ain't like that this time."

The edge returned to his voice, but only for an instant. It wasn't lost on Greg that the kid hadn't called him 'Pig' yet. He took it as a good sign, but didn't let his guard down. The kid took a deep breath, preparing himself to get something off his chest.

"Listen up. I owe you an apology for the stupid shit I said when you came to see me at Juvie last year. Those were my brother Manny's words, not mine."

Greg didn't buy it. At least not yet.

"What's changed?"

"I got into a program. They're training me how to cook, like in a restaurant and shit. It's legit."

Greg winced.

"Sorry if the image of you with a butcher's knife doesn't put my mind at ease."

The kid kicked at the ground while looking up at the evening sky. Greg almost felt sorry for him, but knew he was holding something back. It was right there on the tip of his tongue, practically bursting through his teeth.

"Manny's dead. I'm not fighting his battles for him anymore."

Greg felt all of the angry energy leave his body. He was like a little kid who just discovered the monsters under his bed aren't real. Monsters Greg didn't even realize he was still scared of.

"When?"

"Last week, in a prison fight. I know I said this wasn't over between us, but I was wrong. It's over now, or at least it is for me."

Chapter 10

Greg got up before the sun the next morning. Kristen lay twisted in the sheets beside him; her naked body a pleasant reminder of the night before. They'd talked for more than an hour after he got home from practice, with her laying it all on the line. Greg never considered how hard it must be for her, watching him wander off to his next adventure so soon after the one that brought them together. He was too worried about making a living to realize she felt left behind, stranded with their child in the expanding backstory of his life.

He lay there the next morning thinking about everything she'd said. Greg wondered if he would ever be as honest with her as she'd been with him. Would there come a time to tell her he'd fallen off the wagon, or how jealous he was about Marco and Gabriella? He had his doubts, but for now everything seemed fine between them. That would have to be enough, at least until he got back home.

Greg ran his fingertips through her hair and gave her a kiss on the cheek. Their son stirred in the nursery, either in need of a new diaper or something to eat. He slipped into his boxers and T-shirt and went in to help him. The kid took one look at his father's face and broke out into a massive, reflexive smile. Greg scooped the boy up, taking him into the kitchen to make coffee.

He had about an hour to kill before meeting the rest of the band down at the beach. There weren't many BCC traditions that survived the twenty-year hiatus, but surfing together on the morning they left on tour was one of them. Greg actually looked forward to it since he hadn't been getting out in the water very much these days. He turned the TV on to try and catch the surf report, finding a goofy morning talk show instead. The chipper cohost was interviewing Tommy Thompson who wore a tailored sport coat over a white Oxford shirt and high-end blue jeans. He looked nothing like the person Greg thought he'd gotten to know.

"Congratulations on the success of your bestseller, *Among the Grizzlies*! Why do you think this book has gotten so popular?"

"Thanks. I honestly have no idea why people seem to be gravitating to this story, except it's so raw and real. I'm just the one collecting all the information and putting it down on the page, but the people I'm writing about are truly fascinating."

"Like Magnus *Ursus*? Am I even saying that correctly?"

"Magnus was definitely a tragic character. So flawed and given to fits of unbelievable rage, but there was something else going on underneath all of that. I don't expect to ever meet another person quite like him. Or, at least I hope not."

"How about the punk rock cop? Oh, what's his name—Greg Salem! I read you two actually became friends during the events in your book."

"We definitely did. His story and those of his friends and family are the ones I get the most questions about. I think people can really relate to what he's been through and the tough choices he's had to make to get where he is today."

"Which is on tour with his old band, right?"

"Yep. Bad Citizen Corporation. I believe they start their tour tomorrow, in Santa Barbara. Don't quote me on that."

"Amazing. Do you two still keep in touch?"

"We do. Spoke with him yesterday, as a matter of fact."

Greg reached for the remote, killing the TV. Tommy almost had him fooled there for a minute until he let his real colors shine through at the end. Nobody else on the planet would have caught his little white lie—"Spoke with him yesterday..."—but Greg did, and that's what mattered most.

He carried his sleeping son into the bedroom, intending to lay him in bed with Kristen, but found her awake. She pulled back the sheets when he walked in, motioning for him to put the baby back down in his crib. Greg returned a few seconds later, peeling off his clothes, to join his wife. The rest of the band would have to wait.

৯৹

IT WAS A CRISP morning out on the beach. The sun was up, but it was a few degrees cooler than normal for this time of year. Greg trotted across the cold sand with his wetsuit on and a small surfboard tucked under his arm. He found Jerry and Tina first, up near the lifeguard tower. They were both wearing jeans and sweatshirts with their hoods pulled up. Jerry had his cinched tight around his beer-bloated face, a lit cigarette jabbing out from between thin lips. It didn't look like either of them had slept much, causing Greg to wonder if the label had accidentally hired a couple to come on tour with BCC.

"Glad you guys made it. Sure I can't convince you to paddle out with us? I've got more boards up at the house."

Tina smiled, waving her phone at him.

"I'm just here to take pictures."

Jerry growled something indecipherable, but it didn't sound pleasant. Greg let it go, heading down to the shoreline where JJ waited.

"I thought you were blowing us off."

"Sorry. I was on daddy duty. Where's everybody else?"

JJ nodded to a set of head-high waves breaking in the distance.

"Chris couldn't wait, so he got right in. I haven't seen Marco yet."

"You're his roommate."

"I took a shift at Eddie's last night, to make a little extra cash. He was already crashed out when I got home, and gone when I woke up this morning. I thought he'd be down here with you."

Greg sat down on the sand, wrapping the cuff of the surfboard leash around his ankle. He stood up and took a couple of tentative steps into the cold water.

"You ready? Not much time before we have to get on the road."

Greg knew JJ wasn't a big surfer, but he'd never missed one of these BCC pre-tour rituals. Not even when he was too strung out to take a shower for days at a time. JJ's dedication to the band always impressed Greg, even when everything else about his bassist drove him up a wall.

The two of them pushed their boards out into the whitewash, climbing on when the water got deep enough to paddle. They'd almost reached Chris when he caught a wave, nearly decapitating JJ with the fin of his board as he swooped by. Greg and Chris were both laughing when JJ reemerged a few seconds later, a horrified look on his face.

"Very funny, guys. Not smart to drown your bassist before the first show."

Greg couldn't hold back. Picking on JJ was another one of his favorite BCC tour traditions.

"That's okay, JJ. We never turn your amp on anyway. You're only in the band because of your good looks."

Chris continued chuckling as he paddled out to catch another ride. Greg was a few feet behind him, while JJ seemed content to bob on his board until somebody else said it was time to go in.

Chris went up and over a few shapeless mountains of water before straddling his board between sets. Greg caught up to him, taking the moment to check in on his young guitarist.

"You excited?"

"Hell yeah, but I'm a little bummed my mom has to come."

"I wouldn't worry about it. We'll make sure she gives you some space. Besides, it'll be like having your own personal roadie while the rest of us have to buy our own food and do our own laundry."

"Nobody said anything about doing laundry on tour."

Greg smiled.

"I guess I was kind of reaching with that one, but you get my point. You'll still have plenty of fun. Anything else on your mind?"

Chris shrugged, a sure sign that something was bothering a teenager. Greg gave him a moment to spit it out, pressing the issue when Chris went quiet.

"You got something to say, you should say it now. There's no such thing as a private conversation once we're in the van."

"I don't know. I mean, what do you think about Jerry?"

Now Greg shrugged, a sure sign that a middle-aged beach bum was about to drop some wisdom on you.

"I think Jerry's a hired gun, but you're in the band. So you're basically his boss. Remember that the next time he's giving you shit. Just don't ever tell him I said that or the record label will be pissed at me. Cool?"

"Cool. Where's Marco?"

"No idea. I was about to ask you the same thing."

Chris spotted a wave forming on the horizon, paddling out to meet it. Greg did the same, catching the one right behind it. He carved his way for shore, spotting Marco up on the sand. There was somebody standing right beside him, holding his hand. Greg rode the wave all the way in, unleashed himself and jogged straight for his drummer.

"Good to see you, Marco. Can I have a word?"

"Totally, bro."

He turned around to face Gabriella, giving her a kiss on the lips.

"Wait here with Tina and Jerry, baby. I'll be right back."

Marco seemed oblivious to what Greg might want to talk about, but not for long. They were barely out of earshot when Greg laid into him.

"What the hell is she doing here?"

Marco looked over at Gabriella and back at Greg, realization slowly dawning behind his puppy-dog eyes.

"She showed up at my place last night after practice. It was a total surprise."

"She's wanted in connection with a murder case."

"No way, dude. She didn't have anything to do with that."

"I know that's what you want to believe, but the only thing that matters is Detective Bowers' opinion."

"That's what I'm saying, bro. She was on stage at a warehouse show downtown when the murders happened. There were cameras and everything. She cleared it with BCPD yesterday afternoon, before she crashed at my pad."

Greg wasn't convinced, and did a terrible job hiding it. Marco threw his hands up in surrender.

"Fine. Ask her yourself."

Marco waved Gabriella over. The look on her face made it clear she wasn't in the mood to be interrogated again. Greg took his chances. He waited for Marco to give them some space before launching into her.

"Marco says you have an alibi for the murders."

"Excuse me? Last I checked you weren't a cop any more. And why don't you show me a little respect, I'm in mourning."

Greg swallowed a laugh, in case she was serious. Gabriella wasn't an easy read on the best days, much less a couple days after her husband was brutally murdered; no matter how much she seemed to resent him and all of his success.

"Sorry for your loss. Marco said you were lucky enough to get out of the house before the—before everything happened."

"I was only there for like ten minutes to get some clothes and make-up together. If I knew Marco was waiting for me out front I wouldn't have taken one of Tony's cars. The garages are out near the service entrance in the back alley."

"So, where'd you go?"

"I was rapping at a private party downtown, but that's none of your damn business. The important thing is the security cameras showed me leaving way before that whole mess."

"And now you're back here hanging out with Marco?"

She looked over at his drummer with something approaching admiration on her face. Or maybe she had a thing for middle-aged punk musicians without a penny to their name.

"He's like a tiny rescue dog. A scrawny little Chihuahua."

Greg had never heard a more accurate description of his friend, but it didn't get him any closer to understanding what this hip-hop bombshell saw in him. He was concerned that all of this might really be about his own jealousy. Greg had done many terrifying things in his life, but he'd never lost out on a girl to Marco.

Maybe there was first time for everything.

"You're not coming on tour with us. The van's full."

She flipped her hair back with the tips of her painted nails, rolling her eyes like a teenaged girl.

"Get over yourself. I'm about to be filthy rich. I could fly a private jet to your lame ass shows if I wanted to. Which I don't."

She was right, and he knew it. It only made him want to ask more questions about what she was doing with Marco, and a few about whether or not Tony Flores put a prenuptial agreement in place.

᠙

GREG HAD ONE MORE stop to make before they climbed in the van to leave. Officer Bob handwrote the note Detective Bowers gave him at the station. It explained where Greg could find his old nemesis, and asked him to stop by when he had a chance. Greg thought it could wait until after the tour, but then he looked up the address.

The Dickies plowed through "Fan Mail" as he pulled the El Camino into the Specialty Cancer Treatment facility's parking lot. He left the engine running to let the song play out. Part of him wanted to throw the car into reverse and get the hell out of there, but knew it wasn't an option. Time was running short if he wanted to say goodbye. He had to remind himself that whatever happened on the tour, it was much worse for Officer Bob than it was for him.

He twisted the key, making his way to the front desk. The woman seated there asked him to sign in while she dialed a nurse to escort him inside. Soft piano music wafted from the speakers to match the neutral orange lighting in the waiting room. A small stone fountain burbled gently in one corner. The whole scene made Greg's skin crawl.

His wait was mercifully short. A young man with an intentionally calm voice led him through the security doors and down a long, tiled hallway. Framed posters on the wall featured grainy images of distant sunsets, each accompanied by a life-affirming quote.

They entered a small guest room where Officer Bob sat at a wooden table. He looked up and smiled when Greg walked in, taking the chair next to him. The nurse told them they had an hour before backing out, shutting the door behind him. Greg wasn't sure what to expect from this visit, so he let Officer Bob make the first move.

"I'm surprised Bowers gave you my note."

"Me too. How long have you known?"

Greg studied his face. He didn't look any better or worse than the last time they'd seen each other; just an older version of the man Greg had known for most of his life. Except for the persistent, weak cough dotting his sentences.

"Got the diagnosis last year. Thought I beat it, but then the cancer spread. I'm stuck here until they can figure out how bad it is—or the insurance money runs out. Whichever comes first."

Greg felt the air being crushed from his lungs.

"I'm not really sure what to say…"

"I just thought we should see each other one more time, in case something drastic happens while you're out of town."

"What about your wife?"

Greg felt funny asking the question, since he didn't even know her name.

"She's nearby. Hasn't really left my side in weeks. Not sure I'd go through with any of this if it wasn't for her."

Officer Bob put his hands down on the table, slowly pushing himself up. Greg could see now he was much thinner than before, his clothes hanging from him like secondhand rags. He stood up to help, but Officer Bob waved him off. He shuffled over to the bed to lay down.

"I get dizzy all the time now. I'm so exhausted from all the medication they're giving me."

"Should I go?"

"No. Pull a chair over here. I won't keep you too long."

Greg slid over, suddenly sensitive to every little noise he made.

"I can stay as long as you want."

"Thanks."

Officer Bob closed his eyes. His breathing got shallow. Greg thought the old man might have fallen asleep. He stood up to leave, but didn't get far.

"Have you talked with Bowers again about what happened at Eddie's?"

"More listening than talking, but yes. I was at his office yesterday."

"Be careful with him. He's not a laid-back local like us. And he seems to have a real hard-on for you."

"Then why hire him?"

"Not my choice. I'm just handing off the reins. But he needs your help with this case, even if he won't admit it. He doesn't know this town the way you do. Doesn't understand the people around here."

"He's already made up his mind, far as I can tell. Seems to think a lot like you."

Greg felt like a coward taking such a cheap shot, but he couldn't help himself. The true nature of their relationship revealed, adversarial until the bitter end. Officer Bob brought his forearm up to rest on his head.

"Do you remember the day of your brother's funeral?"

Greg sat down again, shifting to get comfortable.

"Some of it." Greg was relieved to see him smile, weak as it was. "Why?"

"We got a call at the station about a bar fight. I knew it was you right away."

"Me against a couple of bouncers? Not much of a fight."

"I remember pulling up outside and watching you fly through the front door. That was the first time I ever saw you drunk."

"It was the first time I ever got drunk."

Greg felt nauseous reliving that day. Those bouncers worked him over pretty good before they got tired of toying around. He might have been buried right alongside Tim if Officer Bob hadn't shown up when he did.

"I'm still surprised you didn't arrest me."

"You'd rather have been in jail than at the church. I thought you'd regret that decision."

Greg tried to force a laugh, coming up blank.

"You were probably right."

"You said something to me, when I drove you home to get cleaned up. Do you remember?"

"Not exactly. No."

"You told me you would never forgive me for ruling Tim's death a suicide."

"I was just an angry kid. None of it made sense to me. It still doesn't."

Officer Bob opened his eyes, turning his head to look at Greg.

"I wonder if you ever realized that I'm not the one you needed to forgive?"

Chapter 11

In Greg's mind, the drive from The Bay Cities to downtown Santa Barbara should be all coastline. The reality was more like sitting in bumper-to-bumper traffic on the 405 freeway before crawling through the San Fernando Valley on the 101. It used to be they could step on the gas once they were past Woodland Hills, but a new housing development sprang up a little further north every year. Even the once remote canyons were overrun by soccer moms dropping their kids off at over-priced private schools in the drought-choked, piss-yellow hills.

Greg couldn't believe his eyes. The winding grade that dropped northbound traffic down into Oxnard from Thousand Oaks was lined with outlet malls and business parks. He looked out the van's passenger window, trying to figure out when exactly all of these new neighborhoods were built. He'd driven this route plenty of times over the years, either on his way up to surf Rincon or for camping trips at El Capitan State Beach, but he'd never paid much attention to the sprawl. Even Ventura became a desirable beach community when he wasn't looking.

With JJ behind the wheel, Greg was free to explore his thoughts. They were less than a hundred miles north of home, but he could already feel the tour working its magic on his mind. He turned around to take a look at the rest of the crew in the fifteen-passenger van, impressed by the assembled misfits. Chris sat in the row right behind JJ with Junior beside him. They both had buds tucked into their ears, attempting to give each other space while sitting inches apart.

Jerry, Tina, and Marco were holding down the third row. Jerry still had his hoodie on, dead asleep and oblivious that his head rattled against the window. Tina was on her laptop and connected to the van's mobile hotspot, searching for cheap motels, reviewing contracts, and trying to find the quickest route between venues to save gas. One of her main jobs as the tour manager was to always find ways to cut corners and, from the looks of things, she took it pretty seriously. Marco was next to her, staring off into space. Greg guessed he was reliving whatever memories Gabriella bestowed on him the previous night.

Suitcases, backpacks, and other personal effects filled the last row. All of the actual gear—guitars, amps, and drums—were locked up in the trailer they towed. The only thing missing were roadies, but Greg decided they could live without them on such a short tour. For one thing, roadies didn't come cheap. And for another, they were some of the vilest animals on the planet with built-in divining rods for finding cocaine and other kinds of trouble. He thought he'd spare Chris the exposure to that side of the music business for as long as he could—even if it meant setting up and breaking down their own gear for a week-and-a-half. The money they saved allowed them to get their own motel rooms, an indulgence Greg had never experienced as a young man.

He turned back to look out the windshield. Something about the mind-numbing velocity of road life cleared his head. For the next couple of weeks, his job had nothing to do with tailing cheating spouses or cleaning up messes for the local police. It felt good for the moment to pretend like this would be his new life, just going up on stage to perform. Things were stable between Kristen and him, at least for now; he and Marco didn't have any open cases waiting for them at home, and it looked like money might not be as big a problem in the near future.

The sense of calm inside of him was short-lived. Greg's thoughts soon turned to the dead kid at Eddie's. Even thinking about Detective Bowers' words—"copycat suicide"—made him feel queasy. Not only because it meant the BCPD were taking the easy way out on yet another case, but because it reinforced all of their faulty conclusions about Tim's death. Conclusions reached by a man who was fighting for his own life back in The Bay Cities. Greg replayed their last conversation in his mind, trying to figure out what Officer Bob meant when he talked about forgiveness. The more Greg chewed on the riddle, the angrier he got. Nobody deserved forgiveness the way he felt these days.

He looked up a while later, surprised to see they were only twenty miles away from Santa Barbara's State Street exit. That gave them plenty of time to check into their motel before heading over to the club for sound check. It was starting to feel like touring when you're older meant cutting down on the unnecessary bullshit. *If all the drives are this easy, I might book a few more shows before we make the record.*

He felt a tap on his shoulder.

"I have to take a dump."

"Come on, Marco. Hold it. We'll be at the motel in fifteen minutes."

"No dice, dude. I've been holding it since Camarillo. We have to pull over."

JJ flipped the blinker in response, merging to take the next off-ramp. The sudden deceleration brought everybody out of their van-induced stupor. Chris leaned forward to look out the front window.

"Where are we?"

"A little south of Santa Barbara. We're making a quick pit stop, then getting right back on the freeway."

"Cool. You think there's a Starbucks around here?"

"We'll get coffee at the motel. You probably shouldn't even leave the van."

Junior leaned in to join the conversation.

"I'll just grab a quick snack while Marco's in the bathroom. I was so stressed out about packing this morning that I totally forgot to eat."

"They'll have food at the club. We're only going to be here for a couple of minutes, tops. Right, Tina?"

Greg was looking for backup. He hoped an experienced tour manager would be able to provide it. She didn't disappoint.

"Everybody listen up. We're stopping for five minutes. Don't wander too far away from the van."

Greg leaned back in his chair, relieved somebody else took charge of the situation—until he heard Jerry's sleep-thick voice.

"I need a new lighter and a pack of smokes."

JJ hit a red light at the bottom of the ramp. He craned his neck to the left and right, looking for a gas station or fast food restaurant. There was nothing immediately in view, so Tina jumped on her phone to start searching.

"Says there's a Gas Mart four miles that way."

She pointed to her right. Greg couldn't believe his ears. In all his time on the road, he'd always made it a rule to only stop if you could see the signs from the freeway.

"I don't know, you guys. Four miles could take forever. And who knows if they even have a public bathroom. Let's gun it for the motel."

Marco leaned back, panting.

"I'm turtling, bro. We need to find a bathroom right now!"

Tina scooted a few inches away from Marco while Jerry howled with laughter. JJ followed Tina's directions, heading east on a one-lane road winding through the mansions of Montecito. They crawled past several antique shops, a college for photography and design, and a golf store, before they finally saw the gas station fifteen minutes later. JJ brought the van to a stop along a line of pumps and every door flew open.

Pretty soon, it was only JJ and Greg sitting there.

"I think we should fill up while we're here."

"Did you check the prices?"

"Greg, we aren't little kids any more. I think we can afford to splurge a couple cents a gallon if it means not stopping tomorrow on our way to San Francisco."

"Fine. Make sure you keep your receipts."

Greg hopped out. He could see Tina and Jerry inside of the gas station's small convenience mart, but there was no sign of Chris and Junior. He crossed the parking lot, spotting them a block down the street. They were hauling ass for a Starbuck's sign in the distance. Greg considered taking off without them if they didn't make it back in time, quickly surmising he would be the loser in that scenario. If worse came to worst, the van could always swing down there to grab them on the way back to the freeway.

He went inside as Jerry walked out tamping down a fresh pack of cigarettes.

"Heading back to the van?"

"After a few puffs."

"Okay. See you in a minute."

Tina stopped Greg as he made his way to the drink refrigerators.

"Did you give everybody their per diems?"

"I thought you had them. You got the cash from the label, right?"

"Shit. I knew I forgot something. What are we going to do?"

Greg shoved a hand into his pocket, coming back with four twenties.

"Use this, but keep track. I don't want to pay for Jerry's nicotine habit all tour."

"Thanks."

She took the money up to the register to have the bills broken into five and ten dollar bills. Greg pulled the glass door open, reaching for an energy drink when he heard a loud flushing sound. Marco came bounding out of the bathroom door right next to him.

"Close call, bro. I wouldn't go in there if I was you. Got any cash?"

"Just like old times. Talk to Tina."

Marco disappeared. Greg made his selection, heading back to the counter. He paid for his drink and went out to the van. The gas nozzle was still in the tank, but JJ was gone. Then he smelled a familiar odor he'd come to associate with Jerry.

Greg set his bag down on the passenger seat, going around the side of the building. Jerry stood there, taking a small pipe out of JJ's hand. He took one look at Greg and coughed up an enormous plume of smoke.

"I can explain."

"Seriously, JJ? We haven't even played our first show and you're already getting high again."

"It's one hit. Calm the fuck down."

"Calm down? I don't give two shits if you're high all the time from now on. It just means somebody else has to drive."

Jerry pulled the pipe from his mouth, revealing a shit-eating grin.

"I'll drive."

"You're kind of missing the point. And you're already on my nerves. Finish up and let's get out of here."

Greg stormed back over to the van, relieved to see Tina and Marco were back in their seats. That only left Chris and Junior unaccounted for. It was another couple of minutes, but JJ and Jerry eventually ambled back over to climb in as well. Greg climbed behind the wheel, double-checking they weren't about to drive off with the gas pump in the process.

It took him a second to collect his thoughts.

"All right. Here's the plan. We're going to grab Chris and Junior from Starbuck's—"

Jerry leaned forward in his seat.

"I want Starbuck's."

"Shut the fuck up."

Greg turned the key in the ignition, throwing the van into drive. He tried to make eye contact with Jerry in the rearview mirror, but could only see Tina. The look on her face was a mixture of shock and disappointment.

"What?"

"I get it, you want to get to the motel. We all do, but you don't have to be a dick."

"Do me favor, Tina. Tell your asshole boyfriend to keep his mouth shut and everything will be fine."

"Boyfriend?"

They were finally starting to move when Marco jumped up.

"I have to go again."

Greg slammed on the brakes.

"What?!"

"I can't help it. My stomach's all jacked up. Go get Chris and Junior from Starbuck's, then come back for me."

He slid the van door open without waiting for a response. It was barely closed again before Greg stepped on the gas. He could see Chris and Junior making their way up the sidewalk on the right. He pulled over and ordered them to climb in.

Jerry's bloodshot eyes stared longingly at their cups before he started whining.

"Oh, man. I really want Starbuck's now."

Greg ignored him this time, making a mental note to snap his neck when they got to the motel. He was too busy at the moment trying to find a place wide enough to turn around a fifteen-passenger van with a trailer. They had gone several stop lights when he spotted a grocery store parking lot. He wheeled the van in, winding through the maze of tightly packed cars before finding his way to the exit. It was another ten minutes before they finally made it back to the gas station.

They pulled in along the same line of pumps as last time. There was no sign of Marco. Greg brought his forehead down onto the steering wheel.

"Fucking perfect!"

Junior gave him a quick slap across the back of his head.

"Watch your language. You've got a kid in the van."

They all knew Junior was the only one who could get away with that, but it seemed to snap Greg out of his manic spiral. He told everybody to stay put and went inside to look for their drummer. The bathroom was empty. The clerk behind the counter said the last customer left a few minutes ago. Greg ran out to the sidewalk, easily spotting Marco a mile down the road, shuffling toward the freeway on ramp. He got back behind the wheel, catching up with him in no time.

Marco climbed in without saying a word. Greg didn't return the favor.

"You said we should come back to pick you up at the gas station."

"I thought you guys bailed. I was getting ready to hitchhike to the show."

"Don't be an idiot. We wouldn't leave without you."

"Whatever. We should have gone straight to the motel."

&

IN THE END, THEY went straight to the club. Traffic was a mess downtown and Greg didn't want to miss sound check. He thought it would give them one more chance to practice. Nobody said a word as they pulled along the side of the building and filed out. JJ and Marco went straight back to the trailer to start unloading the gear. Greg went around to the front of the building with Tina to see if anybody was in the box office.

The Noise Chamber was a run-down theater only a few blocks from the beach, tucked between two warehouses along the railroad tracks. The outside of the building was lined with corrugated steel siding painted a splotchy shade of purple. All of the doors were locked tight and every window was painted black from the inside. Greg rang the "Delivery" buzzer over and over while Tina stepped back.

She tapped Greg on the shoulder, motioning to the marquee.

"Check it out."

He looked up to see what she was pointing at: "Tonight— Bad Citizen Corporation—Sold Out!"

"Nice. Let's go around back to see if there's a stage entrance."

They almost did a complete loop around the building before they found the door. It was propped open a couple of inches with a wobbly barstool. Greg plunged straight from the warm Santa Barbara sunshine and into the inky subterranean darkness. It only took a second to get his night vision back, just long enough for Tina to forge ahead without him. He saw the rest of the band up on the stage at the other end of the room. They were already setting up the equipment. He headed that way.

Greg walked up the rickety stage steps, making a left to find the dressing room. He pushed through a heavy, velvet curtain and followed a hallway until it split. A white piece of paper was taped to the door in front of him, the letters "BCC" handwritten in black Sharpie. Junior was already sprawled out on the sofa when Greg walked in.

"If you're looking for dead bodies, you're out of luck."

"Very funny. That's the last thing I want to think about right now."

He set his backpack down on the coffee table, eyes wandering around the dimly lit room. It smelled like the walls were recently painted, barely covering years of etched-in band graffiti. A cracked mirror was mounted on one wall between two framed posters from the night the club opened a decade before. He found it funny that this place didn't even exist the last time Bad Citizen Corporation toured.

Junior stood up, walking over to stand beside him.

"Are you all right, Greg? You seem a little high strung."

"Just need to get this first show over with. Everything will be fine if we can get through tonight. I should probably get out there for sound check."

He followed the hallway back to the stage, finding himself face-to-face with Jerry. They hadn't said a word to each other since the fight in the van.

"Has anybody seen the sound guy yet?"

Jerry strummed a loud power chord in response. The jagged tone reflected off the concrete floors, reverberating around the empty rafters before decaying into nothingness. A disembodied voice came from the wedge speakers at their feet.

"Sounds pretty good out here. If you bring the master volume down a little, I'll turn you up in the mix."

Jerry turned away from Greg to follow the sound guy's instructions. Greg edged by him, fairly certain only one of them would survive this little tour. Chris stood in front of the drum riser, tuning his guitar. He shot Greg a glance while frantically fumbling with the pegs on the headstock.

"I can't get this thing in tune!"

"You're just nervous about the show, Chris. We'll play a couple of songs once everything's set up. That should help you calm down."

Greg gave him a fatherly squeeze on the shoulder. He noticed Marco's kit was already set up, but the cymbals were missing.

"I think you forgot something."

"No shit. I'm kind of freaking out. Are you sure we loaded them?"

"They're probably still out in the trailer. Go check."

Marco jumped up, jogging out the back door. Greg watched him go before shifting his attention to JJ who ran scales on his bass. He couldn't bring his bloodshot eyes to meet Greg's stare.

"Is this how it's going to be the entire tour?"

"What's that supposed to mean?"

"You're being a dick. Nobody even wants to be around you."

"Tell you what. I'll stop being a dick once you guys get your shit together."

Marco raced back in with his cymbal case. He sat down on his stool and spun them into place one by one. The disembodied voice of the sound guy came back in the speakers when he finished.

"You guys ready to run a few songs?"

Greg stepped up to the microphone at center stage, taking his position. Chris turned to ask him which songs they should practice.

"All of them."

Chapter 12

Junior swung the dressing room door open.

"Showtime, old man."

Greg raced by her, hurrying down the backstage hallway. He could hear Marco banging on his snare drum and Chris nervously twiddling with his strings. The crowd stomped its feet, chanting the letter's "B-C-C" again and again. A thick-necked bouncer with the words "Event Staff" stretched across his barrel chest was stationed at the edge of the stage. He waved a flashlight to escort the band on without tripping over the tangle of cables at their feet. Greg stopped to take a gulp of water, crushing the bottle in his fist as he bounded into the spotlight. The band kicked into the first song as he lunged for the mic.

The surging mass of bodies roared with approval as Greg unleashed a torrent of lyrics. Words followed words, utterly meaningless to him as they flowed freely from his memory, like a tired actor repeating his lines. He concentrated on the sea of faces in front of him, their lips silently echoing everything he screamed; faces contorted into a blurry, snarling mass of sweat and skin and brightly colored hair. Shoving matches broke out here and there, creating a vacuum in the center of the room that drew the most violent people among them.

Three songs down and Greg was already dripping with sweat. Marco showed no mercy, quickly clicking off song after song. The room got so hot and humid that Greg felt like he glided across the stage, swimming through a thick soup engulfing him in its sloppy embrace. It got so bad that the battalion of bouncers were dragging half-unconscious people from the crush down front. There were a few kids among them, but most of the casualties were men his own age; their shirtless, chubby torsos slick with radiant sweat that gave new life to old tattoos. He guessed they'd come there hoping to recapture a glimpse of their long-lost youth, ending up with a few new bruises and a massive hangover instead.

They were in the home stretch when a handful of young guys fought their way onto the stage. The overworked bouncers didn't have the manpower to defend against the breach, being forced to chase them instead. Soon there were three times as many fans as band members on stage. One by one, the eager fans wound their way between Jerry, Chris, and JJ, kicking and flailing their way to Greg before leaping back into the crowd. Some stopped to pose for pictures with him, hamming it up for the appreciative audience. Others tried to share the mic with him, shouting out whatever lyrics they remembered. One of them leaned over and whispered, "I am Tim" in Greg's ear.

It happened so fast—and Greg was so disoriented from adrenalin-overload—that he couldn't say which one of them said it. He knew it was a guy, shirtless like all the rest, but it was all a blur beyond that. It could have been almost any one of the hundreds of people staring back at him. He scanned the room with paranoid eyes for the rest of the set, barely grunting a "thank you" and "goodbye" before slamming his mic to the floor when it ended. The rest of the band filed off behind him, stumbling like a line of soldiers marching home from war.

Greg reached the dressing room first, kicking the door open with the soul of his sneaker. He stuck his head inside to scan the space before entering all the way. Marco almost plowed into him in his haste to find a clean towel and a cold bottle of water.

"Shit or get off the pot, bro!"

Chris and Jerry followed Marco; each one of them sweatier than the last. Greg kept his eyes on the ceiling as they squeezed by him without saying a word. Any little movement in the room, every shifting shadow, made him think there was a lifeless body swaying gently overhead.

JJ came through the door last, shoving Greg into the room ahead of him.

"Great show! All that practice really paid off."

The rest of them traded high fives, repeatedly congratulating each other. Greg stepped over to the sofa, slouching down against one of the arms and placing a towel over his head. He stayed there until all of his thoughts were quiet again.

৵

THE CLUB WAS ALMOST empty when Greg finally emerged from backstage. The rest of the band had broken down all of their gear and stacked it up in a pile on the dance floor. It shouldn't take long to load the trailer between the five them, especially if Junior was willing to help. Once that was done, they could finally make it over to the motel to get some rest before the six-hour drive to San Francisco the next day.

Greg spotted Tina at the bar, settling up with the promoter. He hoped she got paid in cash so they had enough money to keep the band members afloat. Jerry sat on the stool beside her, sucking down free beer and glaring at his own reflection in the mirror behind the cash register. Greg was heading that way when Junior took him by surprise. She sat up in a booth, grabbing the strap of his backpack to stop him in his tracks.

"Where they hell have you been?"

Greg knew instantly she'd had a few cocktails.

"Taking it easy backstage. Looks like you're having fun."

"I'm kind of on vacation. Where are you going?"

"To the bar. Need a drink for the road?"

"Better not, but thanks. I'll see you out at the van."

Greg went over to join Tina, who was packing her things up. Jerry was already gone when he arrived.

"Where's your boyfriend?"

He tried to be friendly, but the comment fell flat. She slammed her bag down on the bar, looking up at him with an unreadable expression. He realized too late it was only the calm before a serious storm.

"Who the hell do you think you are?"

"Excuse me?"

"I know this is your band and that, at least for now, we all work for you. But that doesn't mean you get to be a bully."

"Sorry. I was just messing around."

"Well, it's not funny. Jerry and I are friends, nothing more. Stop trying to make a big deal out of it."

Greg threw his hands up.

"Okay, okay. I'll back off. Can we talk about how much we got paid tonight?"

Tina reached for her purse, pulling out an envelope stuffed with bills of almost every denomination. Eyeballing it, he guessed they'd raked in close to two thousand dollars.

"Thirty-two hundred and change. Not counting whatever we made from T-shirt sales, which is where I'm headed next."

"Amazing."

"We'll do even better tomorrow night. See you outside in a few minutes."

Greg lingered at the bar alone. The room looked even bigger from this perspective, especially now that it was empty. Thinking back, he couldn't remember ever playing to so many people in Santa Barbara—not even when the band was in its prime. *I guess it helps to have older fans with money in the bank.*

He walked the length of the club, emerging into the brisk night air. A southbound train rumbled by as he took the steps down to the sidewalk. He looked up, seeing the marquee had already been changed to advertise the next night's show. Greg didn't recognize a single band on the bill. He rounded the corner of the building expecting to find Marco and JJ, but the van was locked up tight.

He dropped his backpack to the ground near the front bumper and pulled out his phone. There was a missed call from Kristen. He hit redial, waiting for her to answer.

"Hi, sweetheart. How was the show?"

"Really good. You guys doing okay?"

"Timmy's asleep and I'm sitting here trying to find something to watch. Before I forget, did Tommy get hold of you?"

Greg hesitated for split second, but hoped she didn't catch it.

"No. I don't see a missed call from him."

"It's nothing urgent. He called to say hi and check in on me."

"Why would he be checking on you?"

"He's my friend, too, in case you forgot. Give him a call. He's worried about you."

"Maybe I will. Call you tomorrow."

"Goodnight, Greg. I love you."

"Goodnight."

He ended the call, his thumb still hovering over the keypad. *Tommy should be man enough to call me directly, rather than going through my wife.*

Greg was still trying to decide what to do when the rest of the band walked up. Chris led the pack, his Marshall half stack bumping and skidding across the rocky parking lot. He still glowed from the show.

"Where the hell were you? We've been waiting inside."

"I thought you guys were out here already."

Marco walked by, carrying a kick drum on top of his head. Junior straggled behind him with his cymbal case. Jerry had a guitar in each hand and a cigarette dangling from between his lips. JJ cradled a cardboard box full of "BCC" T-shirts.

Greg grabbed the cymbal case from Junior, going around to join Marco near the trailer.

"How many trips do you think this will take?"

"At least three. Maybe four. Whistle while you work, bro."

JJ set the box down, reaching into his pocket for the keys. Greg reached out to hold the lock for him, but it came free in his hand. It looked like the shackle had been clipped with bolt cutters.

"Crap! Stand back. Somebody broke into the trailer."

Greg slid the latch aside, pulling the door open. The interior was pitch black and almost completely empty since they'd pretty much taken everything into the club.

"We'll have to buy a new lock tomorrow, but I don't think they managed to steal anything from us. Let's load up and get out of here."

He reached for Marco's kick drum. The shocks squeaked and bounced when he stepped onto the bumper. Tina gasped.

"Something's moving in there!"

Greg brought his phone up at the same time as JJ and Junior. One by one they flipped on their flashlight apps, filling the trailer with enough light to reveal the body dangling inside. The noose was tied to an eyebolt mounted high up near the ceiling so his feet cleared the floor. A familiar sign hung around his broken neck.

ℒ

THE SANTA BARBARA PD kept them at the club until almost one in the morning. They'd taken each of them back inside one at a time to ask the usual battery of questions. Greg knew it was a wasted effort since none of them was the killer, but that was a conclusion the investigators needed to reach on their own.

One officer in particular seemed very interested in Greg. His name was Alex Romero, and he looked to be in his early thirties with thick black hair parted neatly on the right. His friendly round face clashed with his muscular frame. Greg saw the fading remnants of several earring holes in both lobes.

"Tell me again why none of you saw the body right away."

"It was dark. We were tired. What's it matter?"

Officer Romero jotted down some notes in his flip pad.

"Might not. Trying to get a complete understanding of the crime scene."

"Has your ME taken the body out of the trailer yet?"

"Should be all clear."

Greg stood and headed for the door. Officer Romero was right behind him.

"You're playing tomorrow night in San Francisco, right?"

"Yep. You a closeted punk fan or something?"

"No doubt. I used to listen to you guys in junior high. Do you mind signing something for me? I've got it out in the cruiser."

"Sure...as long as it isn't a book."

Officer Romero froze. Greg held his ground for a second, before giving the guy a break.

"I'm kidding. Meet me over at the van and I'll sign it for you."

Marco closed the trailer door as Greg walked up. The band must have loaded the gear as soon as the cops got it on a gurney and dusted for prints. *Who can blame them for wanting to get the hell out of here?*

"Go wait in the van with everybody else. I'll be there in a second."

Marco shuffled off around the back of the trailer as the officer approached from the other side. He held his copy of *Among the Grizzlies* out along with a ballpoint pen. Greg flipped to the title page, scribbling a quick inscription along with his initials, then his phone number.

"You ever seen anything like this around here before?"

"This is definitely our first trailer suicide."

There was that word again. Greg slapped the book shut before handing it back.

"What makes you think it's a suicide and not a murder?"

"Good question. I almost forgot you were a cop. I guess it's hard to imagine a motive for something like this."

"Even with a similar death at one of our shows down south?"

Officer Romero tapped the cover of the book with his pen.

"They're calling that a copycat suicide. Besides, I doubt there's a serial killer following your band around on tour. That sounds crazy."

Greg wasn't sure what to say in response. It did seem strange once he heard the officer say it out loud. Somebody would have to harbor a pretty serious grudge to follow BCC around killing their fans. *But the only person I know who hates me that much is supposedly dead.*

"Out of curiosity. If you were going to investigate this as a murder, where would you start?"

"With the band members, of course. You guys are the common denominator. If it's murder, it's either somebody in that van right now or one of them knows who it is."

"Right. Well, enjoy the book."

"Thanks! I've already read it, twice."

Greg went around, climbing in behind the wheel. He shifted the rearview mirror, studying the slumped silhouettes and exhausted faces in the rows behind him. If one of them *was* the killer, this tour would be really short.

Chapter 13

Greg woke up the next morning in the driver's seat of the van. An empty bottle of vodka was wedged between his legs as the sun poked up over the top of the hotel. He reached up to pull the visor down, spewing yellow bile into his lap instead. The clock on the dashboard read 7:00 a.m.

Greg picked up his phone to dial the Police Chief in Virgil Heights. He answered on the third ring.

"It's a little early."

"Is it true about Manny? Is he dead?"

"Christ, Greg. You sound like shit. Please tell me you aren't hungover."

"Still drunk. Answer the question."

He heard a disappointed sigh on the other end of the line.

"I knew this tour was a bad idea."

"Is he dead?!"

"Jesus. Yes."

Greg leaned back against the headrest. He tried to make sense of it all, but his fatigued brain couldn't process the information.

"Did you see the body?"

"What? Of course not. I was here when they called—"

"When's the last time you saw his little brother?

"He was here last night. Why's that matter?"

Greg hung up, carefully climbing out of the van. He had to clean up before the rest of the band woke up. None of them needed to see him in his current state, especially Chris or Marco. He eased his shirt off, tossing it directly into a nearby dumpster. His suitcase felt heavy as he pulled it across the parking lot to the staircase.

The ice machine clunked and chugged as he passed by on the way to his room. He pulled the key card from his pocket, inserting it into the slot. The lock wheezed open and he twisted the lever to go inside. It was the first time he'd seen it since checking in the night before. The perfectly-made bed looked inviting, but he had work to do if he wanted to survive the drive north. He pulled the comforter back and rumpled the sheets in case any visitors stopped by to check on him.

Greg stripped down, taking his toiletry bag into the bathroom. The reflection in the mirror revealed a beaten man. Dark circles shadowed his eyes, recessed deep into his puffy face. A thick white crust caked the corners of his lips, a perfect match to the slimy coating on his tongue. He looked almost as disgusting as he felt, hating himself for wanting another drink. A glass of tap water and a couple of aspirin would have to do.

The small shower smelled of mildew. Greg turned the hot water up until it scalded his skin, scrubbing every inch with sweet-smelling soap. He brushed his teeth, but decided not to shave in hopes the stubble would help hide his pasty skin. The mouthwash waited for him when he stepped out to dry off. He gargled twice and even swallowed a little for good measure. His reflection looked slightly better the next time he checked.

Junior was waiting for him when he stepped out of the bathroom with a towel wrapped around his waist. She sat on the edge of the bed, a cup of coffee in each hand.

"I forgot to get you cream."

Greg took a cup, hoping she didn't notice his shaking hand.

"Thanks. Everything okay?"

"Really hungover is all. Why didn't you cut me off last night?"

Greg managed a chuckle.

"I didn't want to ruin your vacation."

He smiled before taking a sip. She groaned, falling back onto the unused bed.

"I feel like I owe you an apology for teasing you about the suicide, if that's even what they were."

"Don't worry about it. There's still no way to know what's really going on."

"But I am worried, Greg. I'm worried about Chris being on this tour with dead bodies showing up all over the place. And I'm worried about you."

Junior sat up, leaning back on her hands. Her eyes traced the tattoos on his chest for a moment before she turned her head.

"You're not looking so good. Get any sleep last night?"

"Me? I tossed and turned a lot. Hoping to catch a nap in the van."

"That makes two of us. You thinking about canceling the rest of the tour?"

That stopped Greg in his tracks.

"Why? The cops all seems to think these are copycat suicides."

"What about you?"

"My opinion doesn't matter. The cops can solve their own cases."

She stood up and went for the door, turning back before stepping outside.

"You're starting to get a little gut. You should think about doing some sit-ups or something."

"Thanks for noticing."

Greg got dressed and went down to the van, opening all of the windows and doors. He found a pack of Jerry's cigarettes and lit a few, letting them burn on the edges of empty soda cans. It wasn't exactly incense, but it helped to cover the smell of vodka and vomit.

ൟ

"THIS SUCKS, BRO."

They were inching along in afternoon traffic through San Mateo. Marco sat in the passenger seat, his feet propped up on the dashboard. Greg drove again, gripping the wheel until his knuckles went white. He'd worn a baseball hat and wrap-around shades since they got in

the van that morning. Nobody asked how he was feeling or made
sarcastic comments about his profuse sweating, so Greg guessed he
was in the clear. Just in time to start obsessing about his next drink.

"Welcome to Northern California."

"Dude. This traffic is way worse than LA."

"Don't let the locals hear you say that. The club's only a few miles
from here."

The Foggy Bottom stood in the Mission District, a punk
landmark in a sea of burrito joints, craft beer bars, and funky coffee
shops. Unlike in Santa Barbara, BCC had actually played this club on
a few of their previous tours. They were mostly an opening act back
then, in the days when punk shows featured anywhere from five to ten
bands. Tonight they were headlining, with only two local acts on the
bill before them. Greg didn't plan to watch either of them.

"Have you been thinking about what happened last night?"

Marco looked over his shoulder. Everybody else either slept or
had their headphones on. He kept his voice down anyway.

"Like, non-stop. What the fuck's going on?"

"Police are calling it copycat suicides."

Marco exhaled loudly.

"Yeah right, bro. Two shows and two stiffs ain't some co-winky-dink."

"What if it happens again tonight?"

"We need to make sure it doesn't or this tour is dust."

"I'm more worried about finding another body."

"That makes two of us, bro."

The congestion eased up right before they reached their exit. Greg
noticed a lot had changed since the last time he was there. Several of
the pastel-colored apartment buildings enjoyed facelifts, and there
were fewer empty storefronts. Fancy bakeries and vintage boutiques
had replaced rundown liquor stores and junk shops. Taking a look at
the teeming sidewalks, however, he noticed one thing that remained
the same. Despite all of the cosmetic improvements, the army of
junkies and homeless still ruled the streets of this hipster stronghold.

Marco noticed them, too.

"Always makes me wonder."

"What's that?"

"How I didn't end up out there with them."

Greg knew what he meant. There were several years where he half expected to get the call from Officer Bob telling him Marco died. His friend seemed to plummet deeper into darkness every time Greg ran into him back then. And every time he would bounce back, only to go ever deeper. Things had spiraled much quicker with Tim.

"Have you been keeping in touch with Gabriella?"

"You know it."

Marco turned to look out the passenger window. Greg saw his smile in the reflection on the glass.

"I'm impressed. Is it possible Marco Johnson might actually have gotten a girlfriend?"

"Looks like it. About damn time, too."

They pulled up to the club. A series of orange cones had been placed along the curb out front. Everybody else in the van gathered their stuff and got out, leaving Greg alone with Marco.

"You remember how to parallel park a van with a trailer?"

"I could hotwire it, but not sure I could park it."

Marco rolled down his window, leaning out to take a look. His assessment of the situation was bleak.

"We've basically got just enough room to fit, with an inch or two to wiggle. Let's park somewhere else."

"We need to unload the gear, and load it back in at the end of the night. Not to mention what a nightmare it is to park in this town."

"In that case, you better get some KY. This is gonna be a tight squeeze."

Marco got out to move the cones. He lingered on the sidewalk, attempting to help Greg judge the angles. That meant flailing his arms and barking out indecipherable orders while Greg did a painful three-thousand-point turn. The wheels of the van and trailer were still a good foot-and-a-half from the curb, but they agreed it was close enough for rock and roll.

He met Marco near the trailer door to open the replacement lock.

"Go get everybody and let's get loaded."

Bad choice of words, but Marco didn't seem to notice. He disappeared inside, coming back out with JJ and Chris a few minutes later. They began picking gear off the pile Greg had started on the sidewalk.

"Hey JJ, where's Jerry?"

"Says he's too tired to lift anything right now."

"Tell him he doesn't have a choice."

"Tell him yourself."

Greg knew it wasn't a great idea to leave gear unattended in the Mission. He told Chris to hang back, grabbing two guitars to take into the club. The Foggy Bottom was much easier to maneuver than The Noise Chamber because of its shoebox shape, with the stage at the far end. You could only access the backstage area from a door behind the drum riser. There was a long hallway back there with the dressing room on one side and the bathroom on the other. An exit to the narrow back alley loomed beyond that.

Greg set the guitars down and went looking for Jerry. He found him asleep on a long wooden bench that looked like a relic from a local church.

Greg slapped him hard on the leg.

"Get up. Time to bring the gear in."

Jerry swatted Greg's hand away, rolling onto his side.

"Fuck off."

He snored again in an instant. It could have been the hangover, or he might have finally snapped, but Greg grabbed the guitarist's shirt and yanked him to his feet. Jerry's red eyes shot open as he made a weak attempt at a punch. Greg responded with a shove, sending the guitarist to the floor in a heap.

Greg spun at a noise behind him, ready to take on whoever was next. Junior and Tina gaped. He brought his hands down as the tour manager rushed over to nurse Jerry. She looked up at Greg, hatred in her eyes.

"You could have killed him!"

"Take it easy. I didn't even hit him."

Greg turned to leave, but Junior blocked the way.

"I don't know what happened in here, but you better apologize."

"I'll apologize after he helps us unload the trailer."

❧

THE SHOW RAN LATE, thanks to a faulty fuse in the power circuit that kept blowing out. BCC didn't hit the stage until midnight. Greg was still wound up from the fight, singing almost every song doubled over in front of Chris's amp. The veins and muscles in his neck strained so hard it felt like his head might pop off. It would have been a welcome relief compared to the black energy pounding through his veins. He either needed a drink or somebody he could punch in the face for real this time. Nothing in between would suffice.

The rest of the band sensed the hate radiating off of him and wisely kept their distance. Marco made sure no more than ten or fifteen seconds passed between songs, counting the next one in before everybody had a chance to look at the set lists taped to the ground. Chris spent the whole show catapulting himself into the air from the drum riser, like some acrobat on speed. JJ struck a wide stance at the beginning of the first song and spent the whole show in the same position, sawing at his bass strings with intense focus. Jerry faced his amp the whole time, sending buzz saw squalls of feedback through the PA system in wave after distorted wave.

It was the best the five of them had ever sounded together, and everybody in the club knew it. When the show ended, the sold-out crowd threatened to riot unless the band came back for an encore. Greg stood backstage listening to the thunderous applause and manic screeches of joy, deciding what to do. There were three songs they hadn't played, more than enough to placate the mob. But part of him wanted to see what would happen if they didn't come back out. He wanted to know if they would really burn the place to the ground, or if it was all just an act.

Chris made up Greg's mind for him, pushing between two enormous bouncers to get back on stage. The crowd erupted as he plugged in his guitar. He let the feedback ring out until Marco and JJ came up to join him.

Greg watched them for a moment, soaking up the chaos. He turned to Jerry with a triumphant look in his face.

"What do you think?"

Jerry spit in Greg's face before running off to the dressing room. Greg wanted to follow him and finish what he'd started, but took it to the crowd instead. Everything that had been building up inside of him spilled out on the stage during those last three songs—the blood, bile, and betrayal of tortured nights and aimless vengeance. He felt annihilated when it was done, a useless pile of bloody nerves lying in a pool of electric sweat. He didn't even make it all the way back to the dressing room, collapsing instead behind JJ's bass amp while the club emptied out.

Thirty minutes passed before Greg finally had enough energy to stand again. He rose up, shouldering the backstage door. Jerry was at the far end of the hallway, pushing his way through the fire exit. He had a backpack on one shoulder and a guitar in his other hand. They locked eyes for a heartbeat before the guitarist disappeared into the cold San Francisco night. Greg honestly didn't care if he ever saw him again.

He went into the bathroom to splash water in his face. The water ran rusty in the sink while he inspected his face in the mirror. Things looked even worse in the dim overhead light. His eyes were sunk deep in their sockets while his chins seemed to be multiplying. He twisted his head to see if he still had a good side when a loud crashing sound brought him back to reality.

Greg waited to see if it would happen again, but the silence returned. He guessed it must be Marco or JJ grabbing their stuff from the dressing room. The water still wasn't clear enough to drink, but it felt good on his face. He followed up with a wad of paper towels, hastily wiping grime from his forehead and sweat from his armpits. Several minutes passed before he emerged again, fresh from his pirate bath.

He stepped across the hallway, letting himself into the dressing room. The lights were off, but an oscillating fan whirred in the background. He flipped the switch and saw instantly what had made the noise. A chair was tipped over in the center of the room, only inches below the tips of the latest victim's tennis shoes. The sign hanging around his neck was the same as all the others.

Chapter 14

The third gig of the tour was scheduled only blocks from the Dead March headquarters in Portland. All of the bigwigs would be attending, with a private after-party scheduled at an exclusive restaurant in the Pearl District. Greg assumed it would all get canceled after the third body turned up, but he was wrong. Dead March hired a private security firm instead—for both events— assuring the band the show must go on.

That meant the van had to leave San Francisco at eight in the morning if they wanted to be in Portland for sound check. This caused a lot of anxiety for Greg because half the band wanted to cancel the tour all together. Junior was the most vocal supporter of that plan.

"My son's safety is more important than some stupid show."

"It's not like they're killing band members, mom."

"People are dying, Chris. It doesn't matter if they're in the band or not."

Greg almost jumped in, but knew better than to get between Junior and her son. Besides, he had his own complicated feelings about the murders—*if that's even what they are.* He'd been around and around in his head about it, trying to decide if it really could be a string of unrelated suicides inspired by Tommy's book. If so, they all had blood on their hands. If not, they might not make it home from this tour alive. The more he thought about it, the more he felt like a cop trying to solve a case. That was the last thing he wanted.

In the end, Greg decided they should play the Dead March show and cancel the remaining dates if necessary. He even offered to buy plane tickets home for Junior and Chris. That seemed to calm everybody down, especially combined with the promises of increased security from the label—everybody except for Tina, who threatened to quit several times after Jerry left. Greg suspected she hadn't been totally honest about her relationship with their missing guitarist, but he didn't push it.

Tina still hadn't heard from him the next morning and it ate her up.

"We can't leave without him."

Greg almost put a hand on her shoulder, deciding against it.

"Jerry's a suspect in a murder right now. Do you understand?"

"I thought they were supposed to be suicides."

"Whatever it is, the police think Jerry might be involved."

Tears rolled down Tina's cheeks.

"He didn't do anything. He's not a murderer."

"Even if we wanted to wait around for him, the police would never let him leave. They're only letting us go because we stayed up half the night proving we had nothing to do with it."

What he didn't say was that she better hope the SFPD found him before Greg did. He'd had a bad feeling about Jerry since they first met, one he couldn't shake. But Greg didn't totally buy his guitarist as a killer either and it left him feeling at odds with himself. The cop in him wanted resolution, but something deeper down inside of him wanted a different kind of justice.

"I understand if you aren't coming with us. If you are, we're leaving soon."

Junior went over to console Tina while the others finished loading the van. Chris was already strapped into the passenger seat with his phone jacked into the stereo. Greg eyed the empty row of seats toward the back and tossed the keys to JJ. *With Jerry out of the picture, he probably isn't stoned.*

"You drive the first leg. I need to catch up on some reading."

Greg climbed in, stretching out in the second-to-last row. He could hear Junior still trying to talk sense to Tina outside. It honestly didn't matter to him if she came or not, but he'd rather keep her close in case she had answers. If Jerry really was the killer he probably had some help kidnapping the victims and stringing them up. He was physically capable of doing it alone, but didn't have enough time considering all the demands the band put on him.

Greg pushed the thoughts out of his head once again. He slipped his earplugs in right as Junior led Tina into the first row of seats next to Marco. Dick Dale picked his way through the opening of "Misirlou" as the van lurched forward, heading for the freeway. Greg reached into his backpack and pulled out his copy of *Among the Grizzlies*. He turned to the chapter called "I Am Tim," picking up where he'd left off.

If there's one person in the world who was most affected by Tim Salem's death, it's his little brother Greg—but getting him to talk about it is almost impossible. Even twenty years later, the mere mention of Tim's name will get you a mixed bag of responses, ranging from complete avoidance and denial to explosive fits of rage, often ending in violence. "There's a lot of good in Greg, always has been, but his relationship with Tim brought out the worst in him. It's a pretty typical thing for a young boy to try and impress an older brother, but their relationship always had a competitive edge that made them both act a little crazy," said Bay Cities Police Chief, Robert Stanley. "It would be easy to say that Greg ultimately won since he survived, but I'm not so sure. And I don't think Greg is either."

If Stanley paints a picture of an unhealthy sibling rivalry, consider this memory from BCC bassist, John "JJ" Jacoby. "We were driving through Arizona on our way to Las Vegas to play a show. It was after lunch in late summer, so it must have been over a hundred degrees out. Greg was doing most of the driving in those days because he was the only one sober enough. Tim was in the passenger seat next to him playing DJ on the stereo. It was all the usual stuff like, you know, Black Flag, Descendents, Wasted Youth, Social Distortion—that kind of thing.

Greg couldn't help grinning at JJ's story. He'd forgotten all about that day in the desert, the way he and his brother fought one moment and acted like nothing had happened the next. Definitely not a healthy relationship, but the two of them were closer than he would be with anybody ever again. Even when they were trying to kill each other.

"But then Tim pops this cassette in and, at first, we didn't have any idea what it was. It sounded like some crappy boom-box demos with somebody singing really badly. Well, it turns out it was some of Greg's new songs nobody was supposed to hear yet, but Tim somehow got a copy. Marco and I only figured out what was going on because Greg went ape shit, swerving down the highway, throwing punches at Tim and trying to pull over all at the same time. They ended up rolling around in the dirt for about ten minutes before they were both too exhausted to fight any more. And then they just got back in the van and we started driving again. They were all covered in blood and dirt, but acted like nothing had happened."

My first encounter wasn't as volatile, but no less telling. We met at a small biker bar called Pete's in the Angeles National Forest. Greg sat down next to me at the bar where some friends and I were watching Superbike races on TV. It was an informal conversation between two strangers so I wasn't taking notes, but I think he mentioned his brother Tim in the first five minutes. I had no idea this stranger and I would be in a shootout together a few months later, fending off a sociopathic cult leader named Magnus Ursus. But that's a story for a different chapter...

Greg must have been more exhausted than he realized. He set the book down on his chest to close his eyes for a few minutes. The warm sun coming through the window, combined with the monotonous vibrations of the van, knocked him out.

§

The kid in the blue hat set the gun down on the amplifier. He raised his hands and walked away. Greg tried to chase after him, to stop him from making this mistake, but the room kept getting longer. And with every step Greg took, the temperature dropped a few degrees.

Sharp white icicles formed on the ceiling as he trudged across the cold room. The pointy glass daggers got thicker and longer the deeper in he went, until a few of them began to sprout feet. And then the feet began to swing, hundreds of bodies banging into each other overhead in the enormous meat locker...

"Wake up! It's your turn to drive."

Greg sat up, almost head butting JJ in the process. Sun still streamed through the windows, but it felt like he'd been asleep for a hundred years. He stretched and yawned, trying to convince his body to catch up with his mind.

"Where are we?"

"Town called Yreka. Up near state line. You've been out for almost five hours."

"Christ. That's more than I sleep most nights."

"The van's all gassed up for you. Wake me up when we get to Portland."

Greg slid out of his row, trading places with JJ. He saw now they were in a gas station parking lot. Marco was fast asleep with a sweatshirt pulled over his head. Chris slouched in the front seat with his headphones turned up so loud that Greg could still hear what song it was. He guessed Junior and Tina must be inside the mini mart, which meant he still had a few minutes.

Greg climbed out the sliding door and went inside to look for a bathroom and cup of coffee. He found both in quick order, running into Tina on his way back to the van. She seemed much happier than the last time they'd spoken.

"You snore."

"That's what I hear. Did you get any rest?"

"No, but I did get a text from Jerry. He stayed out late with some friends last night in the city. He already called SFPD and set up a time to give a statement."

"And then back to LA?"

"I guess. I was so happy to hear from him that I forgot to ask."

"Good. That should make tonight a little less stressful for you."

"For all of us."

Greg led her back to the van where Junior was strapped in. Chris and Marco hadn't moved an inch. He didn't look, but assumed JJ was already out like a light. He set his coffee in the drink holder, pulling himself up into the driver's seat. His copilot gave a thumbs up as he turned the key and headed north through endless miles of trees.

Greg waited until everybody settled in before tapping Chris on the shoulder. He only took his headphones halfway off.

"What's up?"

"I wanted to check on you. See how you're doing with everything else going on."

"I'm fine. The shows have been amazing and people are being really cool to me. Don't tell my mom, but this woman actually gave me her phone number last night. It was kind of creepy."

"Sounds about right for a first tour. Getting your mind blown is part of the deal. You scared at all?"

"About the hangings and stuff?" Chris lowered his headphones down around his neck, hitting pause on the player. "Not really. I mean, it's like it's happening to somebody else. You know?"

"Not really. Explain it to me."

"It's like they're not connected. We play our shows and do our thing, and there are these other people doing these other terrible things, only it's happening in the same places we are. If that makes any sense."

"It does make sense. I'm glad you don't feel part of it, but keep your eyes open at the club tonight."

"No problem."

He went to pull his headphones on, but Greg had already reached out to stop him.

"Did I ever tell you any stories of when my brother and I used to tour together?"

୨

THEY ARRIVED IN PORTLAND fifteen minutes before sound check that night, which meant no hotel until after the show. The Supernova Theater was much more modern, and better staffed, than The Foggy Bottom. It offered a loading dock in back with a dedicated parking space for the BCC van. A crew of rough-looking stagehands came out to greet them as soon as they opened the trailer door. They carried most of the gear inside without asking for help. That gave Greg and the band time to find the dressing room and get cleaned up before playing a few songs.

Greg was achy, tired, and ready for a shower, but knew they couldn't skip the chance to practice. Chris was the only guitar player in the band now, so they needed to build up his confidence.

"You're doing great, Chris. You know this set better than any of us."

"Whatever."

Chris turned to face his amp, reading over some notes Greg made for him. JJ sidled up in case Chris had any questions. Greg was about to do the same when Tina walked up to the edge of the stage. There were three uniformed police officers with her. A couple of hefty bouncers loomed a few feet behind them, awaiting orders.

"There are some people here to see you."

He could tell by the slight tremble in her voice that she felt uncomfortable around cops. Not unusual in the music business, but to be expected given the body count this tour racked up. Greg jumped down to the floor, extending his hand to the nearest officer.

"Greg Salem."

She was medium height, medium build, and, judging from the comfortable scowl on her face, medium personality.

"Officer Tierney. We wanted to have a word with you before the show tonight."

"That'd be a nice change of pace. I'm getting used to being questioned into the wee hours of the morning."

Officer Tierney's scowl went from medium to high.

"Is there something funny to you about these murders?"

"Is that what you're calling them here? Seems to change depending which city we're in."

"So, I guess it's true. You're an ex-cop who hates cops."

Great, he thought. *Another one who's read Tommy's book. At least she won't ask me to sign it.*

"No. It's just been a tough couple of days. Laughter helps. You should try it sometime."

He only got a twitching eye in response to his comment.

"I wanted to walk you through the security measures we've put in place around the facility. We've got officers stationed near every entrance and exit, and two backstage. We'll also have one plainclothes officer on the floor during the show, and one in the balcony."

"Impressive, but it might be overkill if the SFPD has their man."

He could feel Tina's body tensing beside him. Officer Tierney sensed it, too, her eyes darting between the two of them.

"We haven't gotten any recent updates, but it sounds like the investigation is still very active."

She turned to leave. Greg stopped her with a question.

"Isn't a private security firm supposed to be handling this?"

He motioned to the mountainous bouncers milling around. Every two-hundred-and-fifty-pound gorilla in an "Event Staff" T-shirt looked the same to Greg now.

Officer Tierney kept her focus on him.

"We advised the promoter to cancel this show, but they refused. As did your record label. So we told them Portland PD would be handling security and sending them a bill."

"Smart. What did you need from me?"

"Don't do anything stupid tonight."

"Sort of defeats the purpose, doesn't it?"

The trio of police officers wandered off to continue their inspection of the club, leaving Greg alone with Tina. She was on him in an instant.

"What the hell was that all about?"

Greg brought his voice down, trying to neutralize her aggravation.

"I know he's your friend, but he's still a suspect. The SFPD are going to take this seriously, whether you like it or not. It's nothing personal. Have you heard from him again?"

She took a step back.

"No, actually. I tried texting and calling, but he hasn't responded since this morning."

"Probably busy sweating it out in an interrogation room. We should concentrate on getting through tonight. Just let the police do their job."

The fight in her evaporated, replaced by an air of defeat.

"Before I forget, I checked us into the hotel. It's right down the block."

She handed him a keycard. Greg felt like he'd won the lottery.

"Thanks. I'm going to run down and grab a shower."

"Stage time is ten tonight, but the label execs will be in the dressing room to meet you around nine-thirty. Don't be late."

ॐ

THE CROWD IN PORTLAND was more subdued than in San Francisco, which made the band work harder to win them over. It wasn't easy at first with Chris flubbing a few guitar lines, but they hit their stride somewhere in the middle of the set. Greg tried to be more animated, covering every corner of the stage and playing to the label execs as much as the fans. They even did another encore, although Greg managed to remain standing this time when the show finally ended. If this truly was the last stop of the tour, Greg would be satisfied.

He followed Marco, JJ, and Chris to the dressing room. Tina waited for them there with a few of the label heads. They were smiling from ear-to-ear, congratulating the band on an amazing show. Greg took it all in, ever aware of the police officer lurking in the corner of the room.

The backstage party broke up about twenty minutes later. Everybody from Dead March went over to the private party across town. The sweat-soaked band was supposed to gather their gear and stop by the hotel to get cleaned up before joining them. Greg said several rounds of goodbyes, doing his best to deal with the endless flood of praise. Another ten minutes passed before the band was finally alone. Even the police officer stepped out into the hallway to give them some privacy.

Greg fell back into a wooden chair, raising a bottle of water.

"Great job, Chris. The crowd loved you tonight."

The boy teased his bangs, attempting to cover his eyes. His words were barely more than a mumble.

"I screwed up, like a lot."

Marco walked over to give Chris a pat on the back.

"It's punk rock, little bro. People are paying to see us screw up."

Things went quiet for a moment as the adrenaline slowly drained from their bloodstreams. Nobody spoke for a few minutes, but all of them were studying the ceiling out of habit; looking for the body that might finally take a night off. Marco broke the silence.

"Let's get our shit loaded into the trailer. I want to get over to the hotel and check in on Gabriella before we go to the party."

JJ stood up, walking over to the dressing room door.

"You guys have a standing phone date every night? Things are getting serious. Looks like I might be losing my roommate soon."

"Whatever, dude. Let's get this over with."

Greg felt a pang of guilt for not calling Kristen that often, but decided it was normal. Marco was still in that puppy-dog phase when the entire universe revolved around a particular girl. Greg and Kristen, on the other hand, had already crossed over into old married couple territory. It happened a little too fast for Greg's taste, but he wasn't sure what to do about it—especially so far from home. The thought filled him with dread as he stood up to get back to work.

Once everything was packed tight and locked up, they decided to leave the van at the club overnight. There was no point trying to park it in the hotel structure if it was only a block away. Greg tilted his head to let the light rain fall on his face. It felt good to be outside stretching his legs after a few days of being cooped up in the van and in clubs. He did the math in his head as they trudged down the slick sidewalk. They'd only played three shows, but driven over a thousand miles.

The next venue was in Seattle the following night, another three-hour drive wrapping up the coastal leg of the tour. From there they had a day off scheduled to accommodate for the long haul to Boise. And then onto Salt Lake City, Albuquerque, Las Vegas, Phoenix, and San Diego. None of that would matter unless they got through tonight without finding another body. *So far, so good.*

They made plans to meet in the lobby again in thirty minutes. Marco and JJ had rooms on the fourth floor. Junior and Chris were on the seventh floor. Greg was all alone on the ninth. He stepped out of the elevator, followed the winding hallway and soon found himself at his door. The "Do Not Disturb" sign was right where he'd left it. He slid his key in, pushing the door open. The twinkling nighttime view of Portland spread out before him through the window.

Greg tossed his things onto the desk to strip his sticky clothes off. Showers were a luxury on tour, one he wasn't ashamed to take advantage of—even twice in one day. He rummaged through his suitcase to find his last clean underwear and an Off! T-shirt, setting them out on the bed. He picked up his phone, convincing himself to call Kristen, but decided it could wait.

There was a text message from an 805 area code number he didn't recognize: "It's Romero, from SB. I've got some information about the other night. Call me."

Greg hit the "Call Back" button, disappointed to get voicemail. His message was short and to the point. He set the phone down on the desk along with his other things and went into the bathroom to rinse off. This Dead March party seemed less important to him as the minutes ticked by. He slid the curtain open, nearly shattering the mirror behind him as he crashed backward into it. Jerry dangled from a rope in the ceiling, his lifeless body gently swaying in the circulating air from the fan. Greg didn't have to read the sign around his neck to know what it said.

October 1998—9:00 p.m.

It was past closing time, but Tim still had a lone customer wandering the store. He was a skinny teenage kid with bubbling acne on both cheeks and a spray of bumps for good measure across his chin. His brand new *Never Mind the Bollocks* T-shirt still bore the creases from the packaging it came in, and the chain and padlock around his neck were a little too shiny. The kid thumbed through the new arrivals, deciding between two of the latest pop punk releases. Tim normally loved that new punk smell, but he was jonesing hard and needed to fix. He thought he deserved it after the afternoon he'd had.

"Come over here. Bring those discs with you."

The kid shuffled over with the albums in his hand, setting them down on the counter. Tim made a show of studying the track listings on the backs of each case. He addressed the kid again without looking up.

"You like the Sex Pistols?"

His voice cracked a little as he answered.

"I guess so, yeah."

"Yes or no. There's no in between."

"Yes."

Tim ventured out into the racks. The kid spun in place, watching him work. Tim came back over to the counter, setting a short stack of CDs next to the others. It felt like his blood was turning to ice in his veins.

"How much money do you have?"

"Twenty dollars."

"That'll get you one of the albums you chose. They're both good, don't get me wrong, but I think you need to do a little homework first. It's a big leap from the Sex Pistols to either of those two bands."

The kid swallowed hard, keeping his mouth shut.

"See these five used discs I picked out. They were hand-selected for you, by me." Tim fanned them out. "We've got *Los Angeles* by X— which is playing on the stereo right now; this is *Double Nickels on the Dime* by the Minutemen; *Wild in the Streets* by the Circle Jerks; *(GI)* by the Germs; and *Damaged* by Black Flag. You have any of these?"

The kid shook his head.

"Good. I'm going to give you a choice. Give me your twenty."

He stuck his hand out and waited. The kid ponied up.

"For this twenty dollars you can either have this new record you chose, this *other* new record you chose, or these five used records I chose for you. You've got one minute to decide."

The kid ran his fingers over each of the discs, studying the album titles and cover art. Tim's entire body shook, and an unbearable itch welled up under every inch of his skin. The seconds crawled until they heard a loud crash back in the office. More clattering and a string of raunchy expletives followed the commotion.

"Stay here."

Tim reached under the counter, running down the back hallway with a wooden baseball bat clutched in his fist. He rounded the corner, swinging wildly at the air all around him. There was nobody in the office that he could see, but several boxes full of empty jewel cases had been knocked over. He went to check behind the desk, finding Marco crouched there. It looked like his ribcage might burst through his shirtless, heaving torso.

"What the fuck are you doing in my office?"

"I came by to say hi, but you were busy playing punk rock Willy Wonka. So I decided to hang out back here."

"Crap! Stay here. Don't touch anything."

Tim threw the bat to the floor, letting it bounce end to end in a spastic dance on the tiled floor. The kid was gone when he got back into the store, and so were all seven CDs that had been on the counter. He flipped the top of the cash box open, relieved to see his day hadn't been a total waste. *Plus, I got his twenty bucks.*

He went to the front door, turned the lock, and flipped the "Closed" sign before killing the lights. Marco sat behind the desk when he returned to the office, cooking up a fresh shot in Tim's spoon.

"You can't just come in here to fix."

Marco carefully set the spoon down, drawing the brown liquid through a cigarette filter and into the syringe he always kept in his sock. With the spoon free, Tim took his turn. They were soon nodding out next to each other, their conversation filled with stretched words and long pauses.

"You ever think about playing in a band again?"

"Not with what a nightmare the last one turned out to be."

Marco coughed, his mouth filling with bile. He reached for a Styrofoam cup to expel the foul liquid. Tim didn't bother looking up.

"It wasn't all bad, bro. We had some good times."

"Maybe in the early days. You talked to my brother lately?"

"Once in a while. He's recording an album with some new dudes. They're using the name BCC. He stole that from you."

Tim gave a half-hearted snort, lazily scratching at scabs on his arm.

"Whatever. *I'm* not using it, so it's all his."

Tim pushed himself up, slowly making his way to the stereo. He ejected *Los Angeles*, replacing it with the *Beach Blvd* compilation. The Simpletones were kicking into "Kristi Q" when Marco came up behind him.

"Gotta bail. Thanks for letting me hang around."

"No problem."

Marco lingered, waiting to ask a tough question Tim already expected.

"You think I could borrow twenty bucks? I'll pay you back..."

Funny how that sentence always seemed to trail off. Tim reached into his pocket, producing the twenty the kid had given him. He handed it Marco without looking back.

"Don't spend it all in one place."

"Thanks, bro. Maybe I'll see you around?"

"Maybe."

Chapter 15

Greg couldn't believe what Officer Romero told him.
"We got hold of the security camera footage from outside of
the club."

"Seriously? Why didn't the promoter mention it that night?"

"The promoter rents the place. The owner's the one who had the
cameras installed, but he rarely shows his face at the venue."

Greg steeled himself, trying not to get his hopes up. Nothing
had gone his way since he got home from Portland yesterday. He and
Marco made the drive in sixteen hours straight while everybody else
flew home. Neither of them said much during the grueling trip, each
caught up in their own dark thoughts about how much had gone
wrong during just three shows.

Since then the label called to tell Greg that BCC's recording budget
was frozen until the murders were solved. They said nobody could make
a good record under so much stress, but he knew it was really about the
bad PR. And who could blame them? They were running a business,
after all. Greg understood how tough it could be, especially since Salem
& Associates still hadn't been paid by Tony Flores' lawyer for the work
they did. They needed the money more than ever with the tour cut
short, but Greg didn't expect a check to come in the mail anytime soon.
He thought about having Marco put pressure on Gabriella, until he
remembered she had been the target of their surveillance.

"The threat of a subpoena was enough to make him hand the
digital files over. At least for two of the cameras. He claims the third
one is broken."

"Anything interesting?"

"It looks like our suspects are two big guys. Like weightlifter big."

Greg knew that the suicide theory had just been shattered for good. He got a mental image of Tony Flores' bodyguards. Then he remembered what they looked like with bullets wounds. The memory sent shivers down his spine. *How many dead bodies can one person see before he starts to lose his mind?*

"Okay. Did you get a look at their faces?"

"No. The camera angles weren't very good. They were wearing ski masks anyway."

"And nobody else was with them?"

"If you're asking about your guitar player, there was no sign of him or anybody else in the footage we got. Doesn't mean he wasn't involved. These guys are probably just the muscle."

The Portland PD told Greg there were signs Jerry had been beaten prior to his death. No determination had been made about if it was a suicide, but that didn't rule out Jerry's participation in the events leading up to his hanging. *Did his two goons turn on him for some reason? Maybe he refused to pay them, or didn't live up to his end of some other kind of bargain?*

But Greg couldn't figure out why Jerry would have done it. He was a prickly bastard, and maybe a little weird, but that didn't necessarily make him a killer. Something didn't add up. He couldn't help thinking Tina had the answers.

"I appreciate you filling me in."

"Least I could do for my favorite singer, but let's keep this between us. Once word gets out that this might be a serial killer the Feds will be all over us. The media, too."

Greg couldn't decide which would be worse.

"Thanks, Romero."

"No problem. I got a name for our victim, by the way."

"Keep it to yourself."

Greg slammed the phone down in frustration. He'd done everything in his power to keep from playing the hero, and here he was again;

stepping in to solve the cases for local police departments up and down the entire West Coast. And he wasn't even getting paid for it.

He considered going for a run to burn off the burst of angry energy, but went into the nursery instead. Timmy was fast asleep in his crib, his head to one side and both fists up in a triumphant posture. He looked so innocent laying there in his fleece pajamas with a teddy bear sewn on the front. Greg wondered how old his son would be before the world kicked him in the teeth, and whether Greg would even be there to protect him.

Kristen tiptoed in behind him, resting her head on his shoulder.

"What're you doing?"

"Watching him sleep."

She brought her head up to look at Greg, lips spreading into a shy smile.

"Do you ever think about having more kids?"

Greg wanted to tell her the truth, but knew it would break her heart. He wrapped his arms around her instead, pulling her close. She laid a cheek on his chest and listened to his heart racing.

"Are you okay, sweetie?"

"I'm fine."

ॐ

GREG FINALLY GOT OUT of the house after lunch. Things were going much better with Kristen on the surface, but he felt the foundation crumbling beneath their feet. Whatever desperate attraction had driven them together at Grizzly Flats was getting more elusive as the months passed. Without all of the external forces trying to rip them apart, Greg found it hard to stay interested. Deep down inside he knew if it weren't for their son, he probably would have left already.

He decided to take his mind off of his personal problems by doing some digging on his tour manger. It took a lot of coaxing and a little flirting, but he finally got some info out of the receptionist at Dead March. She told him Tina lived at a Downtown LA arts complex, spitting distance from Grand Central Market. Greg looked it up on a map and thought it might be worth going down there to ask around about her. He decided to bring Marco along for the ride in case he needed backup.

Greg sped along the boulevard, flipping from his favorite AM news station when the reporter started talking about the body count from "the ill-fated Bad Citizen Corporation tour." He parked in the lot at Eddie's and walked a block to Marco and JJ's condo. Their names were on the registry at the security gate, but Greg had the code memorized. He buzzed himself in, taking the elevator to the third floor.

JJ walked out as Greg arrived.

"How was the drive back from Portland?"

"Long. Your flight go okay?"

"Couple hours. Thanks for footing the bill."

"No need for the whole band to suffer any more than it has."

The look on JJ's face was utter confusion.

"You really think Jerry had something to do with all of this?"

"You tell me. You two seemed to get along. What am I missing?"

"I mean, we got stoned a few times. He was a total smartass, but I never got the impression he was violent. Anyway, I'm heading to work. Marco's in his bedroom with you know who."

Greg stepped inside, pushing the door closed with his foot. He hoped the slamming sound would bring Marco out into the living room, but it didn't work. That meant he'd have to knock and possibly walk in on an awkward situation. He went for the bedroom door when it opened to greet him. Gabriella stood there fully clothed, looking anxious to leave.

"Didn't you two get sick of each other on your little road trip?"

She said it in passing, clearly not in need of an answer. Greg watched her traipse into the kitchen before poking his head inside the bedroom to find Marco. He reclined on the bed, nothing but board shorts on.

"You ready to go?"

"Just need to throw a shirt on and find my flip flops."

"We're going downtown, not to some volleyball tournament."

"Fine."

Marco jumped up, groping at a pile of questionable laundry on the ground. He put jeans on over his board shorts, pulling a sweatshirt over his bare torso. His checkered Vans slip-ons were a loose fit without socks.

"Let's do this."

He went straight for the front door without looking back. Greg stopped him.

"Don't you want to say goodbye to your girlfriend? You've been gone for four days."

"Oh, right. Give me a sec."

Marco strode into the kitchen to give her a high five. She fluttered her eyelashes, smiling at him as he turned to leave. Greg couldn't believe they never exchanged a word.

"You two are perfect for each other."

"You know it, bro."

Traffic crawled heading north, but lightened up when they merged east. The sky was clear and blue, sunlight flickering through the tall palm trees lining the freeway. It wasn't long before a cluster of high rises popped up on the horizon like a glowing blue jewel on the flat LA landscape. Greg studied the dark mountains looming in the background, wondering if he would ever visit his cabin again. He doubted Marco would come along if he did.

Greg reached over to pop the glove compartment open. His Glock was in there as usual, along with a couple of envelopes. He took one out, dropping it in Marco's lap.

"It's not as much as it should have been, but that's your cut from the tour."

Marco scooped it up, flipping his thumb across the bills.

"Looks like Marco gets to live indoors for another month."

"Don't talk about yourself in the third person. The other envelope's for JJ. I meant to bring them upstairs earlier, but spaced out."

"No worries. I can give it to him."

"Thanks, but I learned not to trust you with cash a long time ago."

"Very funny, bro. People change."

They crawled along the 110 interchange, keeping right for the downtown exits. It was the middle of the week, so the grid of streets teemed with a unique mixture of business people in tailored suits, shop owners, and tourists. Each of them played a role in the rebranding of these decimated neighborhoods that had risen from the ashes of a crack epidemic. The scars were still there, but Greg had to look a little harder every time he came to visit.

It took a few minutes to locate the address in the maze of one-way streets, and twice as long to find parking. Greg fed the meter and the two of them made their way up the block.

"The receptionist at Dead March thinks she might have gotten another tour already. We probably don't have to worry about running into her."

"So, are we breaking into her apartment then?"

"Not sure it'll come to that. Let's poke around a little, ask her neighbors some questions. Maybe one of them will recognize Jerry."

Marco gave his front pockets a slap.

"Holy shit! I must have dropped it somewhere."

"Come on, Marco. We haven't even been here five minutes."

"Ha! Gotcha, bro."

They walked up to the front door of The Art Colony Lofts. Every extension on the registry was for a studio or gallery, but none of the tenant's names were listed. Greg tried the door. It didn't budge. He stepped back to study the face of the building, scoping the network of rusted fire escapes zigzagging to the roof. Marco had vanished when he looked back again.

Greg's head swung side-to-side, catching a glimpse of his partner as he disappeared in a cafe down the block. He tried screaming for him to stop, disturbing the pigeons poking around at the ground near his feet. *I swear to God, it's like babysitting somebody else's toddler.*

The chalkboard sign outside of the coffee shop read "Re/Hab Cafe." Greg stepped inside and found Marco at the counter, showing Jerry's picture to a female barista with a hard stare.

Greg wandered over to see if she had anything interesting to say.

"We see lots of white boys looking like that around here."

Marco pushed the picture closer to her.

"What about his eyes? You probably don't see that every day."

She pursed her lips, pulling her head back dramatically.

"Are those contacts? Lydia, come check this shit out."

Another young woman emerged through the swinging kitchen door. She had an apron on over khaki pants and a white polo shirt. Greg noticed both of them had elaborate gang tattoos poking out from under their shirts and spreading down their arms. He was too impatient to wait for their answer.

"Has he been in here or not?"

The two women looked up in unison, as if Greg had three heads. Marco nudged him back a few inches with an elbow to the ribs.

"That's my buddy, Greg. He probably shouldn't have any more coffee. Makes him edgy. This guy in the picture is a friend of ours, but he disappeared."

"I recognize him."

Greg's chin snapped up at the sound of the familiar voice. A young man had come out of the kitchen to see what all the commotion was about. He wore a baker's toque and a stained chef's coat, but he would always be the kid in the blue hat to Greg. Their eyes locked, each of them deciding what to do. It was the kid who eventually nodded to an empty table by the front door, indicating for Greg to follow.

They sat across from each other, still reeling from the shock of the chance encounter. Greg did his best to keep the conversation casual and his voice low.

"This the place you were telling me about?"

"Yeah. They got me covering the afternoon shift by myself. I make all the croissants and shit for the next morning."

"Seems like a good program for you."

The kid looked at his fingernails, picking off little bits of dried dough with his teeth.

"Beats getting shot. What the hell are you doing here?"

"My friend and I are actually on a case. There's a woman who lives in the lofts upstairs, but we can't get in. Not that it matters to you."

"They keep their shit locked up tight. Lots of homeboys running around down here. What's she look like?"

Greg lifted his arm a little above shoulder height, not sure what he hoped to accomplish with this awkward conversation.

"She's short, with dyed hair and lots of piercings."

The kid smiled, bearing crooked yellow teeth.

"I know that crazy bitch. We threw her and her ugly-ass boyfriend out of here a couple of weeks ago."

"Was it the guy in the picture?"

He thought it over while studying Greg's face.

"Could've been. You punk rockers all look the same to me, with your funny hair and ripped-up clothes."

Greg looked over his shoulder and saw Marco waving goodbye to the women. He stood up, ready to get the hell out of there, too.

"Thanks. Glad this is all working out for you."

The kid pushed himself up, straightening out his apron. He gave a quick glance to the girls behind the counter, taking a step closer to Greg.

"Hold up. I can get you into the building. Meet me around back, by the dumpsters."

"You sure you want to risk breaking probation for me?"

"Shit. I wouldn't offer if you were still a pig."

Greg caught up with Marco out on the sidewalk, explaining the situation. He left out the part about who the bakery chef was. They followed the sidewalk around the corner, ducking down the first alley they came to. The air heaved with the smell of old trash and fresh piss. The kid waited for them outside the back door of the bakery. Greg did all the talking when they arrived.

"You have a key or something?"

"We do a lot of deliveries to the people living upstairs. This door's for the freight elevator."

"Any idea what floor she lives on?"

"Damn. I gotta do your whole job for you? Try four or five."

"Thanks. I owe you one."

"We'll call it even, for all that stupid shit I said in Juvie."

The kid nodded and let the door slam shut, sending them into darkness. Greg groped at the wall for a light switch, finding one a few steps in. The fluorescent lights flickered to life, revealing a puzzled look on Marco's face.

"What the hell was that all about?"

"I'll explain later."

"You look kinda freaked out."

Greg ignored his last comment as they got into the freight elevator, riding up to the fourth floor. A single concrete-and-steel-beam hallway unfolded before them, lined with industrial-strength doors on either side. A second smaller elevator waited at the far end on the right, the wooden car barely big enough for two people. A single window looked out over the street where they'd been minutes before. They made their way down the line, gently checking doorknobs and reading the studio names as they went. No luck.

Marco stopped to check out the view when they reached the window.

"Hey, I can see your car. Looks like a Hot Wheels from up here."

He lingered for a moment, before taking a sudden step back.

"What's up? You see something down there?"

"It's nothing, bro. I'm no good with heights. Let's start knocking on some doors."

"Not until we know which studio she lives in."

Greg was heading back to the freight elevator when the nearest door creaked open. A tall woman with thick curls emerged, carrying a violin case. She took one look at the two of them and stopped, an exasperated look forming on her face.

"How did you get in here?

She focused on Greg, so he improvised an answer.

"Looking for a friend, but we got turned around."

She adopted a skeptical pose.

"What's your friend's name?"

"Tina Pierce."

"Of course, it's Tina. Should've known by the looks of you two."
She rolled her eyes. "You're on the wrong floor. Go up one more. It's
the studio right above mine, end of the hall. The door's covered in
band stickers. You can't miss it."

"She a friend of yours?"

"I guess so. I bring her mail in when she's out of town, water the
plants. That kind of thing. This neighborhood isn't great, so we look
out for each other."

Greg and Marco exchanged a glance. She pulled her door shut,
stepping across to the small elevator. Marco sidled up beside her.

"You play violin? We're musicians, too."

She looked down at the case in her hand, a small smile cracking
her lips for the first time. Greg wasn't sure where Marco's new charm
came from, but women suddenly seemed enamored with him.

"This is where I keep my paints and brushes."

"Cool. Is that how you know Tina?"

The elevator dinged and the woman stepped in, pushing the
button for the first floor.

"We've done some small gallery shows together, but her stuff's
totally different than mine. More like performance art. You ever heard
of erotic macramé?"

Greg watched as the door slid shut. He tried to stop it a moment
too late, screaming out a last question before the woman disappeared.

"Did Tina have a partner?"

She shouted her response as the car descended.

"Just her boyfriend, Jerry."

Chapter 16

The fifth floor was identical to the fourth, except for the door at the end of the hallway. Every inch of it was covered in band stickers, creating a swirly mosaic design with the glossy shapes. Small circles and squares intersected with rectangular bumper stickers to spell out the initials "T. B." None of it helped them with the deadbolt.

Marco slowly twisted the knob, giving a silent push. It didn't budge. He lifted a hand to knock, but Greg stopped him.

"What're you doing?"

"No way to know if she's in there, bro."

"What happens if she answers? Are we here selling Girl Scout cookies?"

"Let's just say we came to give her cash from the tour."

"I didn't bring her money with me."

Marco pulled his envelope out, waving it in Greg's face.

"Then we'll give her mine."

Greg released Marco's wrist, letting his partner bang on the door. The first round of knocks got no response, so he went in for a second. A minute passed before Marco finally decided nobody was home.

"No dice."

"Thanks for the update."

Greg made sure they were alone before checking the window overlooking the street below. He slid it open, sticking his head out to inspect the fire escape. It fell a couple feet short of Tina's window, which was propped open with a stack of coffee table books.

He looked over his shoulder to Marco.

"Climb out there and see if you can get in that way."

"Fuck that."

Greg couldn't believe his ears. He'd seen Marco take so many crazy risks that it never crossed his mind he might have limits.

"Since when?"

"Like, forever. Makes my legs go all weird when I look down."

"Looks like it's up to me."

He lifted a leg, ducking out onto the fire escape. Cars and pedestrians passed by down below, but Greg knew that nobody looks up in Los Angeles. He went over to the wrought iron railing, carefully leaning over to reach for the window. Getting leverage wasn't easy with his arm extended at such an awkward angle, but he managed to inch it upward. The stack of books fell into the studio with a clatter when the window opened all the way.

Greg waited to see if there would be any response to the noise before climbing over the railing. It felt rickety now that he held on from the outside. The distance to the window looked to be a foot-and-half, but it felt like he had to jump across the Grand Canyon. He tried not to look down as he stretched a foot out to grope for the sill. The tip of his sneaker found the edge, chips of old paint floating down to the sidewalk below.

Greg firmly planted his sole before reaching out to grip the frame with his hand. There was no going back once he leaned forward. He counted to three in his head before shifting his weight in that direction. His shoulder caught the corner of the window frame, messing with his balance for a terrifying moment before he managed to tumble inside.

The awkward landing sent him skidding across the concrete floor. He recovered and managed to stand, but quickly got tangled in something dangling from the ceiling. Panic overtook him as he imagined Tina's feet clinging to his shoulders and the sides of his head. Greg swatted at the black nylon groping him, thrashing to disentangle himself from the nightmare overhead. He fell to the floor again, grunting and gasping as he scooted away. The distance allowed him to see the device for what it was—a well-used sex swing.

Greg leapt up, desperate for a place to wash his hands—or maybe take a shower. Frantic eyes scanned the cluttered space. Towering shelves lined exposed brick walls, the unfinished wood bowing under the weight of thousands of books, a solid-state stereo, and an impressive collection of CDs and vinyl albums. The small kitchen looked hastily shoved into one corner like an art installation or an afterthought. A ratty futon couch and two coffee table milk crates were the only functional furniture.

It took a beat to spot the bathroom, obscured as it was by ceiling-high stacks of cardboard boxes. He was headed that way when Marco pounded on the front door. Greg went over to let him in.

"Keep it down."

"I heard somebody coming up in the elevator, bro. Thought it might be Tina."

Greg froze.

"Was it?"

"No idea. They got off on a different floor."

"Perfect."

Marco let the door click shut behind him, giving the studio a once over.

"What a dump. I thought artists had good taste."

"Ease up, Marco. I've seen some of the places you've lived in. Take a look around while I go wash my hands."

Marco stood near the sex swing when Greg came out of the bathroom a minute later. One of the coffee table books that had propped the window open was in his hands. Greg looked over his partner's shoulder. The text was all in Japanese.

"What is that?"

"Some kind of bondage book."

Marco flipped to a full-page photo of a naked woman in the throes of ecstasy. She was strung up like some fly in a spider's web, held in suspended animation by an intricate series of ropes. A grey-haired Japanese man stood behind her, a look of pure ecstasy on his wrinkled face. Greg flipped the cover closed to look at the title: *Shibari.*

"What the hell's that mean?"

"I'm thinking 'kinky rope sex.' Check it out."

Marco nodded to a video camera mounted on a tripod, the lens trained on the ceiling. A folding ladder lay on the ground beside it. Greg looked up at the sex swing again. He noticed the eyehooks holding it in place weren't the only ones. Several of them dotted the ceiling across the room, bundled coils of rope hanging from each one.

Greg went over and flipped the screen open. He hit the rewind button, letting the file roll back to the beginning. The screen stayed black when he hit "Play," until a glaring light slowly filled the frame. It revealed a very naked Tina suspended in mid-air, arms tied behind her back with countless knots. The ropes were gracefully looped around her body, immobilizing her ankles and wrists before racing up to a metal ring overhead. The camera pulled back, exposing a silent crowd seated on the floor beneath her. They looked on in awe as Jerry sent her restrained body into motion.

"Holy shit, dude. Those two had a serious rope fetish."

"And only one of them is still alive."

Greg reached out to hit "Stop." A loud banging came from the front door right at that moment. He brought a finger up to his lips, imploring Marco to keep quiet. They backed up toward the window when somebody started yelling out in the hallway.

"Tina! Are you in there?"

It sounded like the woman they'd met on the fourth floor. Greg guessed she'd had second thoughts about the two strangers in the building and come back to check on Tina. He motioned for his partner to get out onto the fire escape. Marco didn't budge, his whisper becoming a hiss.

"No way. I'm staying right here until she leaves."

"She probably has a key."

"Then I guess we'll have to run."

More pounding on the front door, twice as urgent this time.

"Tina! I need to make sure you're alright. I'm coming in, okay?"

A key slid into the lock on the front door. Greg crouched down, stepping out of the window. Marco watched him go, a defiant look on his face. Greg reached out, sliding an arm around his partner's neck to yank him outside. He slid the window shut right as the front door cracked open.

"Tina?"

Greg got Marco to his feet, pushing him up the ladder.

"What the fuck, dude?"

"Keep climbing. Don't look down."

It was only two stories to the roof. Marco went up and over the lip of the building, falling onto his back. Greg stepped over him, heading for the staircase that would take them down to the first floor. He flung the door open and stepped inside, calling out to Marco as he disappeared into the stairwell.

"We have to get out of here before the cops show up."

৯

TWO HOURS LATER. GREG and Marco were stuck in standstill traffic a few miles from The Bay Cities off-ramp. They made it back to the El Camino without being spotted by Tina's neighbor or getting arrested, but had been in traffic ever since. The drive home took twice as long as the drive there. Neither of them had spoken a word in the last fifteen minutes, silently gazing out of their separate windows instead—Greg looking east, Marco looking west.

Rocket from the Crypt chugged through "On A Rope" a few minutes later. Greg's head swam with thoughts about the kid in the blue hat. Without him they might never have found out as much as they did about Tina, but their interaction had a chilling effect. He didn't doubt the kid was getting his act together and trying to move on. Greg just didn't want to feel like he owed him anything. Their lives were already too intertwined.

He decided to give the Police Chief in Virgil Heights a call when he got home. They'd already had a couple of conversations about this subject, but neither of them ended very well. Greg hoped this would be a good excuse to bury the hatchet with his old mentor. If nothing else, it might allow him to get some real sleep. Any relief was welcome the way things had been going recently.

It seemed as if Marco could read his mind.

"You plan on telling me what happened back at the cafe? Looked like you were about to shit yourself when that cook came out of the kitchen."

Greg sighed, choosing his words carefully.

"He wasn't just some cook. That was the kid I shot when I was still a cop."

Marco spun around in his seat, his long hair falling into his eyes. The look on his face was equal parts horror and disappointment.

"Why the hell didn't you tell me?"

"It didn't seem like the right time to get into it. The whole situation's pretty complicated."

Marco retreated, shifting his gaze down to his phone.

"It's cool, bro. We've all got our secrets."

He punched out a few words with his thumbs and scrolled down. Greg heard some sort of video playing, but couldn't tell what it was. Marco didn't keep him in suspense for very long.

"Holy shit. Tina has a ton of videos online. Look at this."

Greg caught a glimpse of her suspended from a different configuration of ropes before shifting his gaze back to the cars all around them.

"Send me the link. I'll watch it when I get home."

"I bet you will!"

Things got quiet again after that. Marco went back to staring out the windshield as they made their way down the ramp. He looked to his right, spotting a familiar car in the parking lot at the rehearsal space.

"What's Junior doing over there?"

"Probably dropping Chris off to play some guitar. He's the only member of the band who actually enjoys rehearsing."

"Tell me about it. He drags JJ down there sometimes, too."

Greg snorted. If music felt like a chore before the tour, it was the last thing he wanted to think about at the moment.

"Can't remember what it feels like to love music that much."

"Come on, bro. We used to be like that. They practically had to tear us away from our gear."

"And now it's like pulling teeth to get us together. Should I drop you off at home?"

"For sure. Gabby's probably getting tired of waiting around for me. Chick loses her mind if she's cooped up too long."

Greg went right a block before Eddie's, pulling up in front of Marco's building.

"I'll give you a call later on. I'm going to do a little more research on Tina and Jerry. We should probably plan on getting together tomorrow."

"Sounds good, bro. Catch you later."

Marco was about to slam the door shut. Greg's arm shot out to stop him.

"Ask Gabriella if she can help us get that money her husband owed us. The bank account's looking ugly."

Marco frowned. It was an expression Greg hadn't seen him wear many times before.

"Seriously? I can't ask my girlfriend to make good on that debt."

"But you've got no problem sleeping with her?"

Marco ignored his comment, fury filling his eyes.

"He hired us to follow her around, bro. In case you forgot."

"You don't have to say any of that. Have her talk to that lawyer. Did you ever figure out his name?"

"What? I told you, it started with 'T.'"

"Very helpful."

"Whatever. Later."

Chapter 17

Greg reached the end of the block before realizing he still hadn't given JJ his tour money. He went right on the boulevard, eyeing the liquor store as he passed. There wasn't much standing between him and a non-stop bender these days, except his own fears of where it might lead. He stopped at Eddie's instead to see if his bassist was still on the clock. The parking lot was packed, but he squeezed the El Camino into a tight spot.

Greg felt like a tourist stepping inside. He didn't recognize anybody behind the bar, and most of the crowd was younger than him by at least a decade. Music blared from the jukebox, pool balls cracked, and the hum of conversation filled every corner of the room. It was a familiar scene Greg had experienced a million times, but it felt like somebody else's party now.

He wound through the crowd, looking for JJ back by the stage. He was surprised to find Gabriella there instead, sitting alone at a table in a darkened corner. A half-full martini glass sat in front of her, an empty one beside it. He walked over to make sure everything was all right.

"Happy hour?"

She looked up with an angry expression that quickly dissolved into a sticky smile. Her eyes danced up and down Greg's body.

"It just got a little happier. Sit."

She toasted him before taking a sloppy gulp. Greg watched her, unsure what to say. *She's either drinking to mourn her dead husband, or looking for somebody to take his place for the night.*

Either scenario was a nightmare for Marco.

"Have you seen JJ?"

Greg made a show of looking around the bar for his bassist again. She giggled at his terrible performance.

"He's around here somewhere. That dude's always hanging around in the background when I'm at their place. He's kind of a creeper."

"Speaking of which, Marco's back at home now. Why don't you let me drop you off over there?"

Greg stood up to leave, but Gabriella didn't move—except to finish her drink. She slid the empty glass across the table.

"One more and I'll let you take me home."

She tossed her hair back, licking her lips in the process.

"To Marco's, you mean?"

"Whatever."

Greg went to the bar, shouldering in between two burly men. The bartender worked her way down the line, doing a double take when she reached him.

"Holy shit, you're—"

He held his hand up, palm first. That shut her up.

"I need one more of what the woman over there is having."

He motioned back to the stage without looking. The bartender rose up on her tiptoes, straining to see who he meant.

"All I see is an empty table."

Greg turned in time to watch Gabriella disappearing through the side door. He dropped a twenty on the counter—unsure if she'd paid for her previous drinks—before chasing after her. The sidewalk was already empty when he got outside. He followed the building around to the parking lot. Gabriella was perched on the hood of his car, a high heel up on the bumper to reveal plenty of leg. She was applying a fresh coat of lipstick when Greg trotted up.

"I thought you wanted me to buy you a drink."

She shoved the compact into her bag.

"I was thinking of something a little closer to your place."

Greg laughed it off, but images of her naked body at The Cliffs flooded his mind again. He took a step back, trying to keep his cool despite the sweat forming under his shirt. The last woman who'd hit on him this hard washed up on the beaches of South Bay the next day; the latest victim of Magnus Ursus. That memory replaced the one he tried desperately to ignore, giving him a little distance from the teetering temptation swaying right in front him.

"I think you've had enough. I'll take you back to Marco's. You two can continue the party over there."

She rose up, running the tips of her fingers down his chest.

"Come dance with me, Greg."

Greg opened the passenger door, letting her climb in. He took his time walking around the car, trying to catch his breath. It was only a couple blocks back to Marco's, but he knew it would be a long ride.

Greg jumped in, keeping his left shoulder against the window. She sensed the distance between them, dropping a hand on his thigh.

"My place up on the cliffs is empty. Maybe we should drive up there and go skinny dipping."

"It's also a crime scene, in case you forgot."

Sometimes nothing worked better than a cheap shot.

"That's not what my lawyer says. He told me to move back in whenever I want."

"Who's this mysterious lawyer of yours, anyway?"

She leaned in, working her hand up his leg.

"Stop trying to change the subject. I know you want to rock this body. There's no use pretending like you don't."

She had a point, but he'd never admit it—least of all to her. He only hoped Marco would survive this night. Whatever sent her into sexual overdrive, his partner was about to feel the full impact. Greg was more than a little envious.

It felt like an eternity before they pulled up outside of the building. Greg left the engine running while she swung her feet out to the pavement. Gabriella glanced at him over her shoulder, wild hair trailing down her back.

"You could always come upstairs and join the party."

"Maybe next time."

❧

"Chief, it's Greg."

Complete silence on the other end. Greg tried waiting him out, but couldn't pull it off.

"Come on. You wouldn't have answered if you didn't want to talk."

This was met with the sound of rustling paper. Greg took that as progress.

"I'm calling to apologize. For the last time I called. I didn't have any right to talk to you like that. I'm sorry."

The Police Chief in Virgil Heights cleared his throat. Greg went silent, sure the old man was about to speak. Painful seconds ticked by before Greg gave it one more shot.

"Listen. I understand why you're pissed off at me. I let you down… again. I thought you'd be used it by now, but—"

"Knock it off with the charming school boy act. You let yourself down, not me. You're a grown man, Greg. Act like it for a change."

"So, you *are* there. I meant what I said. I know I've been a prick."

"A selfish prick's more like it."

"Fair enough, but I've been under a lot of pressure. I mean, the tour got canceled because some psycho's following us around, and things aren't going great with Kristen."

"So you decided to start drinking again instead of asking for help. 'Poor me, poor me, pour me another drink.'"

Greg winced. He never liked when people quoted twelve-step literature to him, especially not when he needed to hear it the most.

"I called to tell you I ran into the kid with the blue hat."

That got the Police Chief's attention.

"What? Where?"

"Downtown. We were on a case and accidentally stumbled into the place where he works."

"He looks different, doesn't he?"

"I guess. He definitely seems to be throwing himself into that program. Think it'll stick?"

"I hope so. Beats ending up like his brother."

Greg choked up at this. In all the time he'd spent worrying about the kid in the blue hat—the sleepless nights when he haunted Greg's dreams—it never crossed his mind they had so much in common; both growing up under the influence of older brothers who led them down dangerous paths. Greg might never have spent time behind bars, but he'd been living in the shadow of Tim's decisions his whole life.

In that moment, he truly hoped the kid wouldn't be doomed to the same fate as Manny or Tim.

"You still there, Greg?"

"Thinking things over."

"Is that all you were calling about? I meant what I said, you know. I don't want to be part of your life unless you get your shit together."

"That might be a while."

"Well, hurry up. I'm not getting any younger. And if we don't talk again, I hope you find a way to take care of yourself."

"Chief, hang on. I—"

The line went dead.

৽

DETECTIVE BOWERS WAS LEANING on the hood of a police cruiser when Greg pulled up to the back of his house. He rolled the El Camino to a stop right in front of him, the bumper only inches from his kneecaps. Headlights shined in his emotionless face, but he didn't flinch or seem to care.

Greg shoved the paper bag under the passenger seat. Detective Bowers launched in before he even got out of the car.

"Were your ears burning?"

"They ring a little, but that's about it."

"Funny guy. I had an interesting call with a few detectives in Santa Barbara, San Francisco, and Portland. Your name came up several times. Lots of differing opinions about you floating around out there these days."

"Thanks for the update."

Greg went to open the gate. Detective Bowers blocked his path. A new fire burned in his piggy little eyes.

"We're combining resources to investigate the homicides."

"You mean you're finally going to do your job?"

"Careful what you wish for. The FBI's been sniffing around. You might be in deeper shit than you realize."

"I'd be more worried if I thought you actually had something on me, which you don't because I didn't do anything."

"Don't get cocky, asshole. We went over all of the available evidence from the four crime scenes. Took almost two hours on the phone, but we finally came to a solid conclusion. All roads lead back to you and the band."

Greg wanted to bring up the security camera footage from Santa Barbara, but thought it might be a trap. If it was, he wouldn't let himself be tripped up so easily. And he wouldn't risk Officer Romero's badge just to win a back alley pissing match. Whatever point Detective Bowers was making, Greg would have to be patient.

"It makes perfect sense. The five of you were the only ones at every show. That's a pretty colorful cast of characters you put together, by the way."

"We had a tour manager, too. You might want to look into her."

"Ms. Pierce is on the list of potential suspects, but she's nowhere near the top. There's actually somebody else who's gotten our attention."

Greg got the feeling Detective Bowers was finally ready to drop whatever bomb he had hidden. If the BCPD was being as lazy as usual, he guessed they'd be going after Marco soon. He only hoped his partner wouldn't have to spend all night in jail before they finally came to their senses and cleared him.

"Are you aware of your guitarist's police record?"

This caught Greg off guard. *How can you question a corpse?*

"I honestly never got to know Jerry very well."

Smugness brought a little life to Detective Bowers' face. It looked like he'd finally gotten one up on Greg.

"Not Jerry, you idiot—Chris. We already sent a car over to his house. They're bringing him in for questioning."

"He's a kid, for Christ's sake."

"If it wasn't him, it was somebody else in your band. Maybe it was you."

Greg laughed. It might be better than throwing a punch, but not nearly as satisfying. Detective Bowers stepped forward, sensing Greg's frustration.

"You want to hit me? Go ahead. It's the last thing you'll ever do."

"I'll pass, for now."

"Smart choice, pussy. There's no place for beach trash like you around here anymore."

Greg's head swam. He tried calling Junior the minute Detective Bowers drove away, getting her voicemail instead. There was no point in leaving a message, so he called Eddie. More of the same. He paced around the alley—trying to make sense of every crazy theory he'd just heard—when he remembered the bag tucked away in his car. He raced over to unlock the door, diving across the bench seat to retrieve it. The cap on the bottle gave a satisfying *crack* when he wrenched it open. He was still laying down when the first drop of vodka touched his lips. It hit his tongue in a bitter rush before scorching a trail through his chest.

His empty stomach tightened when the alcohol hit it. He rolled over onto his back, feet sticking out of the open door. The soothing poison hit his blood stream, a warm flush travelling up his neck and spreading across his cheeks.

Greg thought about Chris at the BCPD station, getting worked over by Detective Bowers. He wanted to drive down there and save him from the worst night of his life, but knew he was powerless. His days of easy access to the local police were over, especially with Officer Bob out of the picture. All he could do was wait. He knew Junior and Eddie would be parked in the lobby at the station all night. Greg planned to stay right where he was, away from the people who might try to get between him and his booze.

He sat up, bringing the bottle to his lips again. The brown paper crinkled in his fist when he took another pull. His cheeks felt numb as he swished the clear liquid around, savoring the sickly burn. He stood up to push through the back gate, stumbling into the garage. It felt like coming home. He locked the door, drew the blinds, and left the lights off. The darkness engulfing him paled in comparison to the darkness he craved.

Chapter 18

G reg rolled over, knocking the empty bottle to the floor. It bounced and skidded, spinning to a stop. The high-pitched, hollow sound drew unwanted attention to his skull-crushing headache. He groped blindly for a glass of water, finding a second bottle of vodka instead. The sound of the cap cracking was twice as sweet the second time around.

He struggled to sit up, bringing relief to meet his lips. The thick coating on his tongue lessened the sting, but it still tasted like failure flowing down his throat. The first drink soothed his throbbing temples. The second cleared his mind. The third would have to wait until after the nausea passed.

Greg's phone started ringing across the room, but he ignored it. The early morning sun poked through a crack in the blinds as his head dropped back down to the pillow. He rolled to his side, grabbing Tommy's book. It'd sat on his lap the previous night, begging to be opened. He resisted the temptation then, but felt compelled to read more now—in the golden moment between being hungover and staying drunk.

He opened to the dog-eared page in the "I Am Tim" chapter, his eyes landing on a random paragraph.

The final BCC tour ended sixth months after their second album was released. In that time, they traveled across the United States and Canada seven times, zigzagging all over the map to play more than one hundred and fifty shows. Suffice to say everybody in the band was exhausted,

S.W.

but nobody more so than straight-edged Greg; by the time they got back to Southern California, the other members of the band had all developed serious heroin addictions. Of the three, Tim was reportedly the worst. "Dude had some kind of built in radar for dope. We'd be playing a random basement show in the middle of nowhere and he'd disappear for an hour or two. But he always came back with the goods. Of course, that didn't mean he was willing to share," said Marco Johnson.

To say the relationship between Greg and the rest of the band was strained would be a gross understatement. They stopped communicating completely, right at the moment they were supposed to be getting ready to make a third record. So Greg took matters into his own hands, working with new manager Mikey Fitzgerald to carry on without Tim, Marco, and JJ. Fitzgerald was a high school friend who got a business degree before deciding to try his hand at management. He would go on to marry Greg's high school sweetheart, Edie "Junior" Williams. They had one child together, a son named Chris.

Although Fitzgerald managed BCC prior to Greg deciding to go solo, his influence was not really felt until after the last tour. "Mikey never liked Tim. He was a fast talker, always hustling for a quick buck. Christ, I still can't believe I fell for it," Williams said. "Mikey really wanted to make a name for himself. He thought people like Tim were obstacles. I don't think he ever really cared about Greg's career, it was just an easy way to make his mark."

Greg soon stopped talking to the rest of BCC at Fitzgerald's urging, all while hiring a new line-up of musicians. This perceived betrayal hit Tim right between the eyes. "These days everybody talks about Tim like he was some junkie messiah, but that couldn't be further from the truth. He was a screwed-up kid with a serious drug problem, trying to hold his life together like most of the rest of us," Williams said. "What happened to him—whatever you want to believe about how he died—it happened because of the life he led, the decisions he made. Any one of us could have ended up like him and that's who you'd be asking these questions about now. I remind myself of that all the time; one wrong decision, a little bad luck, and I am Tim."

Greg let the book fall to the floor and took a pull from the bottle. He was sitting up when the garage door swung open. Kristen loomed there, Timmy on her hip.

"There you are. I've been trying to call you all morning."

Greg said nothing. He dragged the back of his hand across his lips, wiping the last of the vodka away. She took one look around the room and burst into tears.

"This is what you're doing now? Wallowing in your own misery out here while your family's inside worried sick about you?"

Something about the way she said "family" felt like a punch to the gut. He wanted to comfort her, tried to stand, but his legs were like rubber. The baby wailed as Greg fell back down to the sofa. He heard the hurt in her voice receding as the anger rolled in.

"Say something! Tell me what the hell you're doing out here."

He attempted to speak, but the words wouldn't come. Mercifully, the baby's crying filled the painful silence. Kristen backed out of the door, slamming it shut behind her.

Greg grabbed the bottle. It was the only response that made sense.

ço

"WAKE UP!"

Greg forced his eyes open a moment before the fist hit the side of his head. He sprang forward, trying in vain to defend himself. A palm met his chest, sending him back on his ass.

"Sit down. You don't stand a chance."

Junior hovered over him, an angry scowl on her face. It didn't look like she'd been sleeping well either. He rubbed at the painful welt forming on his temple; sure that vodka wouldn't be an option for the moment. Neither was getting up.

"What time is it?"

"Time for you to grow the fuck up."

"I get it. You're disappointed in me. Why do you—?"

"*Disappointed* in you? This isn't some soap opera, Greg. Your wife's inside packing her things and getting ready to take off with your son. My son spent the entire night at the police station. *My thirteen-year-old son!"*

Images of Detective Bowers flashed in Greg's mind, his words ringing in Greg's ears. Paralyzing remorse gripped him. Junior swung again, her open hand connecting with his left cheek. The blow stung his bones and rattled his teeth, snapping him back to reality.

"Whatever drama you've got going on means nothing to me now."

Greg could see Junior gearing up to attack him again. He put his hands up in front of his face, waiting for the next blow. It probably wasn't a fight he could win on his best day.

"Is Chris home now?"

Junior calmed down slightly at the sound of her son's name. She took a step back, hands on her face.

"He's with my dad. I told him to get some sleep. Which is what I was trying to do when Kristen called me."

Greg scanned the tables and chairs around him, trying to locate the bottle of vodka. He wouldn't be surprised if it was empty considering how he felt, but he suddenly needed to know. It came as some relief when his foot bumped against it on the floor. That tiny splashing sound meant relief was nearby, as soon as he got rid of Junior.

"Are you going to hit me again if I ask you what time it is?"

"I should." She shook her head in disgust. "It's ten in the morning, okay? And you're still shitfaced, you pathetic fucking loser."

Greg could think of only one thing to say in response.

"I am Tim."

"What are you talking about?"

"I read some of Tommy's book. Those signs—the ones that say 'I am Tim'—they're because of you."

Recognition slowly dawned on her face. It was quickly replaced with a psychotic mask of fury. Greg wondered if he'd live to see lunch, as if he could eat anything without throwing up.

"Are you trying to say this is my fault?"

"No, not the murders. But those signs? That's because of something stupid you said about my brother."

"I didn't say it about your brother, I said it about my friend. But it doesn't matter. I didn't come here to listen to your pathetic excuses for why you fell off the wagon."

"Then why did you come here?"

"To tell you Kristen and Timmy are coming to stay with me. At least until you get your shit together."

"What if I don't want them to come back?"

Junior looked at him as if he were a stranger.

"Then I guess you'll get to spend the rest of your life with the person you love the most—Greg Salem."

URGENT KNOCKING ON THE garage door. Greg stumbled from the sofa, nearly falling on his face in the process. He pulled himself up on the edge of the desk and managed to find the knob.

Gabriella stared back at him when he opened the door. She gave him the once over, wrinkled her nose, and extended a hand. The edge of a white envelope was only inches from his face. She pulled it back before he could snatch it.

"Aren't you going to invite me in?"

He stepped aside.

"Knock yourself out."

She sauntered into the destroyed room with all the attitude of a runway model. Greg was still too cross-eyed to fully appreciate it. He went back over to the sofa, collapsing down into one corner. She slid her sunglasses off, setting them down on the desk along with the envelope.

"Got anything left to drink?"

Greg leaned forward, groping at the floor near his feet. The mostly empty bottle was in his grip when he sat up again. He took a slug before extending it to her.

"Pretend it's a very dry martini."

"My imagination isn't that good. Take a shower and we can go out for a real drink."

Greg sniggered, pointing to the desk.

"I'm not going anywhere. What's in the envelope?"

"It's a check from my lawyer. Payment for the job you did for my—" The words caught in her throat. It was the first time Greg had seen her look vulnerable. "For Tony Flores."

"You mean for following you around?"

"If that's what you want to call it."

"Most guys would follow you around for free."

"Thanks for finally noticing."

Gabriella reached down with crossed arms, shimmying out of her shirt. Her lacy black bra came undone with the flick of a wrist. She leaned forward, pushing her skirt and panties to the floor.

"You ready for that shower yet, or what?"

Greg stayed put despite the sudden urge to get clean. He wondered how many men she'd ruined with her perfect body. Joining them seemed like his fate, unless he kept her talking.

"Your husband threatened to kill me because he thought something like this might happen."

"He was real smart. Be a shame to disappoint him."

She strode forward, naked save for high heels. Greg felt his heart beating for the first time all day. The thick, sludgy blood turned to lava in his veins.

"You're supposed to be in mourning."

"Consider this denial."

"Did you have anything to do with his death?"

If his question offended her, she didn't let it show.

"He was a powerful man with a lot of powerful enemies."

"Men you slept with?"

"I'm young and I like to have fun. I won't apologize to anybody for that. Let me show you what I mean."

She planted a soft kiss on the nape of his neck. He felt his futile resistance melting. Only one card left to play before all bets were off.

"What about Marco?"

She took him by the hands, lifting him up.

"I won't tell if you won't."

He followed her into the bathroom, drinking in the view as she bent over to turn on the hot water. Steam rose up all around as she reached out to undress him.

It took every ounce of strength in his body to push her away.

"I can't. It would destroy him."

She stepped forward, her lips caressing his ear.

"I thought you were a bad boy."

Greg stepped back, his body rigid.

"You really have to go."

Gabriella stormed out of the bathroom, grabbing her clothes from the floor as she went. Greg listened to her cursing him as she made her way across the room. He waited until she got dressed before closing the door. He turned the lock and stripped. The scalding water felt good against his sticky skin, washing away the sweat and grime of the last twelve hours. They swirled down the drain along with the fresh memories of Gabriella's naked body. *There has to be some kind of award for resisting that much temptation.*

He stayed under the water until she was gone. His legs were still a little wobbly as he dried off, but his head felt clearer than it had in days. He wrapped the towel around his waist and went back out to the sofa. The room was empty, but the white envelope rested on his pillow. He picked it up, seeing the note scribbled on the outside: "I took the check with me. You know where to find me if you want it."

Greg dropped the envelope onto the desk, right next to his phone. There were several messages waiting for him, but he needed to make a liquor store run before he dealt with any of that.

He'd barely stepped away to get dressed when the phone rang. Greg looked at the name on the screen before picking it up.

"JJ?"

"Holy shit, Greg. You have to get down to the rehearsal space right now."

"Why? Is everything all right?"

"There's another body. Somebody's hanging from the ceiling."

Chapter 19

Greg pulled up to the rehearsal space minutes after the police cruisers. He saw the flashing lights and got overwhelmed by the urge to leave. There was nothing he could do to help JJ, especially in his current condition. The assembled BCPD officers would probably take one look at him and slap the cuffs on for drunk driving. Even if he looked better than he felt, the evidence of his most recent bender was written all over his face—dark circles, bad breath, and fresh sweat. A quick peek at his shattered reflection in the rearview mirror confirmed it.

Greg dropped the El Camino into reverse, slowly backing out. He slammed the brakes on when he heard a loud slap against his tailgate.

"That's far enough. Get out of the car."

He put her in park, but left the engine running as he opened his door. Detective Bowers waited for him to emerge.

"Leaving us so soon? The party's just getting started."

His brain felt like a smooth stone as he fished for an excuse.

"I, uh, just came down here to grab some gear."

"Okay. Now I know something's up." Detective Bowers studied his face, quickly sizing him up. "I was surprised you didn't stop by the station last night to try and save your little guitarist. At least I was until I got a good look at you. Rough night?"

"I'm a little under the weather."

"You're actually hungover, and maybe still drunk. I'd love to field test you right now, but we've got bigger problems. What do you know about this situation?"

Greg was caught between lies and he knew it. He'd have to come clean if he wanted to get out of there.

"Nothing much. JJ called me when he found the body."

"He called you before he called us? Interesting."

Detective Bowers put his hands on his hips, looking over his shoulder at the crime scene. Greg saw JJ in the doorway of their room, an officer on either side of him. They both had notepads out, peppering him with questions.

"Do you know anything about the victim?"

"Well, his name was Tim, if you believe the sign around his neck. Beyond that, I was hoping you or your friend over there could shed some light."

"I was at home all morning."

"Alone?"

Greg hesitated, unsure if the visits from Kristen and Junior were even real. He had no doubt about Gabriella, but that one would be the hardest to explain.

"I had company. I'd be happy to share who once you tell me why you're so convinced the killer is in my band."

A scowl formed at the corners of Detective Bowers mouth.

"You're friend's son, Chris, is off the hook—for now. Your tweaker friend Marco was next on the list, but I think we'll move JJ to the front of the line. If they both check out, we'll be coming for you. That's a promise."

"What about our tour manager?"

"Leave Ms. Pierce to us, and all of the other police work while you're at it. We'll be talking very soon."

Detective Bowers charged toward JJ to take over the interrogation. Greg got back into his car, tracing the boulevard back to the beach. He passed Marco's condo along the way and considered stopping by, but wasn't sure he could look his friend in the eye. Not with all of the impure thoughts about Gabriella still dancing around his mind. At some point, Greg would have to tell Marco what kind of woman he was mixed up with. Not today.

Greg needed something to take the edge off, followed by sleep. He rolled by Eddie's, continuing west until the ocean spread out before him on the horizon. A few waves would probably do wonders, but it was also a lot of work. And he didn't want to risk running into any of his sober friends in his current condition. His liquid salvation would have to keep coming from a bottle, at least for today. He pulled into the next liquor store parking lot, going inside to acquire his remedy.

Greg was relieved to see no police cruisers were waiting for him at home. He grabbed the Glock from the glove compartment, tucking it into the back of his pants as he climbed out. There were a lot of uninvited guests stopping by these days, and not all of them were friendly.

The bag in his hands was twice as full as the last one. He opened the back gate and briefly considered moving the party into the house, but opted for the garage instead. *No need to pollute another environment.*

Greg was so focused on his next drink that he didn't immediately notice the woman sitting on the back deck. Of course, it could've had something to do with her size.

"I heard you stopped by my studio."

He jumped back at the sound of her voice, almost dropping his precious cargo.

"Tina? I thought you were on tour."

"I was, but only for a couple of dates. I've been laying low other than that, trying to figure some things out. Why were you looking for me?"

Greg pushed his way inside, nodding for her to follow. He shoved the bag down under the desk, stashing it back behind the chair. That drink would have to wait until after she left, or as long as he could stand it.

Her eyes looked red and swollen when he saw her in the light, as if she'd been crying for days.

"I'm not really in the mood to hang out, Greg. Tell me what you want and let's get on with our lives."

"You lied to me about your relationship with Jerry."

Her face turned to horror at the sound of his name.

"He's dead, in case you hadn't noticed. Forgive me if I don't see why any of that matters now."

"Because of how he died. Your neighbor told me about the performances you two used to put on. Marco and I looked some of your videos up online. You tie a strong knot."

"For your information, *Shibari* is an ancient Japanese art form. And it's got nothing to do with those murders. If you don't believe me, ask that asshole detective. I just came from his office."

"Detective Bowers? How did he track you down?"

"He didn't. I called them once I heard you were snooping around. I have nothing to do with any of those murders, and I'm getting pretty tired of you telling people I do."

Greg couldn't decide if Tina was innocent or a criminal mastermind. His brain was too fried to form a solid opinion at the moment.

"Look, Jerry and I used to be a couple. We broke up a year ago, but kept working together for my performances. We decided a long time ago not to act like more than friends whenever we were on tour together."

She seemed to be on the verge of tears, but did an admirable job of holding them back. Greg sensed a moment of weakness and pounced.

"Who would want him dead?"

"I could ask you the same question. Detective Bowers seems pretty convinced it was somebody in the band. I have to say, after the fight you and Jerry had in San Francisco, I'm thinking he's right. None of you assholes ever gave him a chance."

If the best defense is a good offense, Tina was a wizard-level strategist. Greg couldn't find a way to shake her, leading him to the conclusion she might be innocent after all—as much as he didn't want to believe it. The alternatives were too terrible to consider.

He went over to the desk and took out a thick envelope.

"This is your cut from the tour."

She tore it open and started counting. Greg hoped she'd count fast. He suffered every second until she left, his mouth watering in anticipation of that first taste of vodka.

She shoved the money into her pocket, looking up at him.

"What about Jerry's cut?"

"What about it?"

"He doesn't have any family. I need money for the funeral."

Greg went back over to the desk, producing a smaller wad of cash. "He only played two shows, so there isn't as much. Do whatever you want with it."

She didn't thank him or say goodbye before disappearing into the bright afternoon sunlight. Greg set the gun down on the desk next to his phone. He grabbed the bag, straight back to getting numb.

స

DARKNESS HAD FALLEN THE next time Greg came up for air. He sat up on the sofa, a sound inside the house dragging him from his stupor. His head felt stuffed with used gauze as he sat in silence, waiting for something else to happen. Whatever came next, he had some decisions to make. His Glock was nearby if it were burglars—or worse. But if it was Kristen, back to collect some more of her things, he needed to stay silent until she went away again.

Then he heard the voices. It sounded like two men were having a conversation in his kitchen, but too quiet to make out what they were saying. He stood up, grabbing his gun before heading outside. The door creaked open. He poked his head around the corner to get a better look. His view was obscured, but the conversation was unmistakable. There were definitely two men inside of his house talking about the latest murder at the rehearsal space. He heard little snippets of their conversation—"Detective Bowers is barking up the wrong tree," "we need to make sure we've got back up," "where they'll find the next body"—but he couldn't identify them.

He crept along the edge of the garage, trying to get a better idea what he was up against. Then he heard something that almost made him laugh.

"Chick's got balls, bro."

Greg relaxed a little at the sound of Marco's voice. He still wasn't sure he was ready to face him, but it didn't look like he had much choice. Greg went back into the garage for a last drink and to stash the Glock before stepping into the house for the first time in a couple of days. Marco sat at the kitchen table when Greg came through the living room, Eddie in the chair across from him. They took one look at the condition Greg was in and both dropped their eyes to the table.

"What the hell are you guys doing here? I thought we were getting robbed."

Eddie went to stand, but Marco waved him off.

"Kristen asked us to swing by. She needs a few things for the baby."

"So, you let yourselves in?"

"She gave me the key, bro. We were actually sitting here trying to figure out if we should wake you up."

"I'm up now."

Eddie kept his mouth shut up to that point, but couldn't hold back any longer. He jumped up, pounding his fist on the table.

"You look like crap. I don't know what the hell's going on here, but you're letting a lot of people down."

That one stung, but Greg did his best to hide it. There were only a couple of people in the world he truly respected and Eddie was one of them. He couldn't decide what hurt more—his words, or the pained look on his face. Greg was in no condition to defend himself, so he attacked instead.

"Maybe it's time people around here stopped relying on me to fix all their problems."

Eddie's face flashed red. Marco leapt up, inserting himself between them.

"Both of you need to chill out. We didn't come here to fight. Kristen asked for some help, but we aren't picking sides. If anything, we want to make sure your family's taken care of until you deal with your bullshit."

"Spare me your junkie logic, Marco. Get whatever you came for and get out."

"Come on, bro. You're the reason Eddie and I are sober. You expect us to let you flame out like this?"

"For the last time: you, your sobriety, and anything else you're dealing with are not my responsibility. Take care of yourselves for a change."

Greg turned to leave. Eddie lunged, grabbing the back of his shirt. The momentum carried them into the living room, Greg tumbling to the ground with Eddie on his back. The old man growled in Greg's ear while Marco clawed to pull him off.

"You don't get to drink yourself to death because things aren't going your way. We aren't your responsibility, Greg—we're your friends. Your family, godammit."

Greg rolled to his side, bucking Eddie to the floor. Marco helped the old man stand, pushing him back into the kitchen. Greg pulled himself up on the edge of the entertainment center. His chest heaved and his body ached.

"You have one minute to get out of my house!"

Marco stepped forward, placing a hand on his shoulder. Greg slapped it away.

"I saved your life and this is how you repay me? Leave."

Greg went out onto the patio while they gathered some things for Kristen and Timmy. It could have been the adrenaline pumping through his veins, but he was overcome with a sudden desire to see his son again. To hold him in his arms and tell him everything would be okay, even if it was a lie.

Eddie came outside with a bag of clothes, brushing by Greg on his way to the back gate. He reached the garage before turning around.

"I'm sorry about what happened inside. Things got out of control."

Greg forced a smile.

"It's okay, Eddie. You won't lose any sobriety points for jumping me from behind."

"I'd punch you right between the eyes if I thought it would help."

"Worry about yourself."

Eddie disappeared into the darkened alley right as Marco emerged. He had Timmy's favorite stuffed animal in one hand, and a stack of board books in the other. It crushed Greg's heart to know he was too drunk to see his own son.

"Please don't tell Kristen what happened here tonight."

"Whatever you say. It's not like she can get any more bummed out at you."

"What about you, Marco? Are you bummed at me, too?"

Marco shook his head, carefully forming his response.

"Greg Salem and I will always be cool, but I could do without the asshole standing in front of me right now."

"What if this is who I am now?"

"Then I guess this is goodbye."

Marco went into the alley to join Eddie. Greg waited until he heard their car drive off before stumbling back into the garage. He strangled the bottle, jamming it into his mouth. The vodka trickled down the sides of his face before he finally slammed it back down on the desk. Gabriella's envelope grabbed his attention.

He picked it up, studying the note she had written. The jagged buzz washing over his brain delivered easy memories of her naked body. And with them came the realization that he might truly be a free man again, with no obligations and no allegiances. If Marco wasn't willing to accept what Greg had become, then there was nothing stopping him from taking Gabriella up on her enticing offer.

Greg decided he'd resisted the inevitable long enough. He went into the bathroom to rinse off and put on some fresh clothes. But first another pull from the bottle. It was a long drive up to her house on the cliffs. He only hoped she'd have a drink waiting for him when he arrived.

ↀ

THE FRONT GATES OF the Flores Estate were wide open when Greg pulled up. He'd made most of the drive with one eye open and both windows down. The fresh air and forced concentration made him feel almost human as he pulled up along the curb. Unfortunately, doubt began to creep in as well. Greg sat behind the wheel for several minutes, weighing his options.

Greg knew he'd sleep with her if he went inside. There was no other reason to be there, and he was only human. But there would be no coming back from it. Marco might be a super bro when it came to supporting his friends, but even he had his limits. Sleeping with his girlfriend topped the list.

The whole situation had gotten so out of control that Greg found himself laughing alone in the darkness of his car, high on the cliffs, with the rest of his life on the line. He laughed so hard that he started to cry.

There were so many people he could call, but he'd already disappointed all of them. Junior, Eddie, and the Police Chief in Virgil Heights—every one of them had always been there for Greg, and he'd let them all down. Even Chris and JJ, two people who needed him the most, were suffering the consequences of his choices. Worst of all, he'd turned his back on Officer Bob when he might be dying.

But it was the thought of Kristen and Timmy that made his blood run cold. He'd abandoned his own family, frozen them out completely. And now they were with Junior, probably trying to decide how to move on without him. *The sad part is, they'll probably be better off.*

Greg wiped the tears from his face and pushed the door open. A cold wind whipped across his back as he walked up the driveway to the house. He could see the lights on inside, every window on the first floor lit up like a shopping mall. There were a couple of sports cars parked in the driveway like usual, but the helicopter was gone. He stepped up onto the porch and rang the doorbell. The chiming tones echoed through the cavernous rooms, but nobody came to answer. It offered another chance to change his mind—to make the right decision—but Greg was committed.

He went around to the side of the house, edging his way through the rose bushes and sculpted hedges. It seemed like an eternity before he rounded the corner leading to the backyard. He'd only gone a few yards when he heard splashing sounds in the distance. Things would go fast if she was already naked when he arrived.

The edge of the dancing blue water came into view when he heard her laugh. He stopped, listening to see if she was out there with anybody. His stomach dropped when he heard a man laughing along with her. Greg told himself that it might be a bodyguard, but knew better. This whole thing started with a job he never wanted to take, and now here he was—ready to destroy his entire world for one night with a woman who already had a date. *How desperate can you get?*

Greg reached the edge of the building, pressing his back against the cool bricks. He poked his head around the corner, spotting her in the hot tub. Her wet hair was slicked back with a drunken smile spread across her face. She squirmed between the two frat boys Greg and Marco had saved her from in the hotel room at The Cliffs. One of them had an arm around her bare shoulders, the other kissing her neck. It didn't look like she needed any saving tonight.

Greg breathed an involuntary sigh of relief. He turned around to leave, walking straight into the barrel of a gun. It was in the grip of a hulking silhouette slowly emerging from the shadows. There was something familiar about the man standing in front of him, but Greg didn't get the chance to figure out what it was. A second man came up behind him, bringing the butt of his gun down across the back of Greg's head. The blow sent a jolt of pain down his neck and into his back as he collapsed to the ground. The follow-up kick made the lights go out.

Chapter 20

Jagged bolts of pain shot through Greg's body, snapping him from his stupor. His head ached from the blow, a stabbing pain amplified by the dull throb of sustained alcohol consumption. Even with his mind swimming in clouds of confusion, Greg knew he was in serious trouble. He was standing upright, for starters, hands tied behind his back. An unwelcome weightlessness undermined his balance whenever he moved his feet, at odds with the noose around his neck. Soft music played somewhere in the background, a cruel soundtrack to his precarious situation.

Greg tried to relax, fighting waves of panic swelling inside of him. Whatever piece of furniture was just below the soles of his sneakers—*A chair? A barstool? A stepladder?*—it wobbled and shifted in response to the slightest movement, threatening to collapse all together. He did his best to stay absolutely still, fighting the urge to release the terrified screams building up inside of him.

Sweat and condensation from his hot breath accumulated in the plastic bag over his head, clinging to his face and choking out the air. It felt like he might drown in his own bodily fluids, if he didn't accidentally hang himself first. He couldn't decide which would be the worse way to die. *Unless they plan to let me suffer before putting a bullet in the back of my head.*

Anything could happen and there was nothing Greg could do to stop it. He didn't even get to fantasize about being rescued since nobody knew where he was. Whatever horrors came next, he would have to endure them alone.

This mental balancing act raged on in his head until a high-pitched whining made it impossible to think at all. The squealing, screeching feedback dragged on so long that Greg half considered kicking off himself, and getting it over with. And then, as suddenly as the noise had come, everything went silent again. But only for a moment.

"Sorry about that, Greg. Tony always ran the mixing board."

Gabriella's voice boomed from every corner of the room. Greg at least knew where he was now—in the pool house recording studio. He clung to the revelation like a life vest in shark-infested waters, certain it did him no good.

"Testing one-two. Can you hear me in there?"

Greg nodded, unsure if she could see him or not.

"I'm glad you found the little note I left for you. Sorry you decided to take me up on my offer when I already had a date. Or two."

She laughed into the microphone, the increased volume giving heavy undertones to her taunting giggles. Greg listened carefully, unable to tell if anybody else was in there with her. He only heard the sound of her rhythmic breathing.

"You want to make a record Greg? The microphones are all plugged in."

"Won't be easy with this bag over my face."

"Good point. I'll have one of my homeboys take it off."

A large hand grabbed his shoulder while a second hand tore at the plastic. Dirty fingernails dug into Greg's skin while ripping a hole to free his face. He gasped as the air flowed in, like emerging from under a huge wave. Gabriella's words sounded like the voice of god coming through the speakers once his ears were exposed.

"Don't get carried away out there. That stool you're standing on has a couple screws loose."

Greg looked around the room. Not much had changed since the last time he was there. Amps and drums were set up for recording all round him, but he was the one in the spotlight. He scanned the room for Gabriella, finding only a soft orange shape on the other side of the tinted mixing room window.

"Why am I up here like this?"

"Isn't it obvious? You're gonna die like the others. Just like your brother died."

Greg's fear collided with his anger, producing a bravado that would only get him killed faster.

"What the hell do you know about my brother?"

"I know what everybody else knows, thanks to that book. Your friend Tommy really seems to like writing about you. Too bad he couldn't be here to take notes now."

It was the first time in months Greg wished Tommy was there. But not Tommy the bestselling author—Greg wanted the gun-wielding Tommy who fought at his side during the shoot out the previous year. The Tommy who got on his motorcycle and chased Magnus Ursus and his men down the mountain, almost losing his life. That Tommy could get him out of this predicament. Unfortunately, he was probably doing a television interview or having dinner with a movie producer instead.

Greg knew there was little chance he'd get out of there alive. His only hope was to buy time until his luck changed.

"What the hell is this all about?"

"You're supposed to be a smart guy. Figure it out."

Greg tried, coming up blank. He guessed that Marco had stumbled onto something bigger than a cheating wife, but that's as far as he got. Then he remembered the two young men he'd seen in the hot tub with Gabriella earlier.

"Those two guys from the hotel. They were never really going to hurt you, right?"

Her laughter echoed around the room.

"Hell no. They're a couple of actors I hired so you could play the hero. Imagine how surprised I was when it was Marco who stepped up instead."

"He learned from the best."

"No doubt. He worships the ground you walk on. It's too bad, though. He's twice the man you'll ever be."

Greg flashed to the last exchange he had with his partner, gnashing his teeth at the ugly memory. Regrets wouldn't matter soon, but he hoped Marco could forgive him. Eddie too. He knew they would in time. That thought gave him comfort, even as his legs began to shake.

"Was that scene at the hotel some sort of twisted sex game you and Tony liked to play?"

"Nope. That was all my idea. Well, me and my homeboys..."

Images of the two bodyguards raced through his head. He could still feel the barrel of the gun pressed against his forehead, the crushing blow against the back of his skull. But it triggered another memory too, something he'd practically forgotten about until that moment.

"The two thugs who pistol whipped me. They were on the security camera footage from Santa Barbara."

"*Now* I'm impressed. Took you long enough. But they weren't just at that show..."

Greg thought about the shows they'd played; remembered the imposing bouncers wandering the clubs every night. They were supposed to be there protecting him and the rest of the band, but it turns out a few of them were hired killers. He wondered if they were hovering nearby at the moment, waiting for the signal to kick the stool out from under his feet—the final stop on their murderous tour.

Greg wished his hangover would go away so he had more brainpower. Another drink would do the trick too, but it also might screw with his balance.

"Why go to all the trouble? You could have killed me and gotten it over with."

"That would be too easy. It's way more fun to watch your whole world fall apart all around you. We had no idea you'd make it so easy for us."

"Who's 'we'? You and Tony?"

"That fool didn't even know what hit him. All I had to do was flash my tits and everything he had was mine."

"So, you *did* kill him..."

"I couldn't get the money unless he was gone, so I crushed him like a roach. Besides, I got tired of putting out for such a dirty old man. He was into some weird shit."

Greg tried not to think about what she meant, his imagination running wild anyway.

"What does this have to do with Marco?"

Gabriella released a long sigh. It trailed off into an awkward moment of silence.

"He was my way of getting close to you, but now he'll have to die, too. All of your friends will, one by one."

"You didn't have to involve him. You could have gone straight to me."

"I told you, Greg, we know a lot about you. We knew it would drive you crazy to see your best friend score a hot piece of ass. It worked perfectly."

"Your loss. He fell for you."

"All of them do, but all they want's my body. Nobody around here knows where I came from, what I've done to get to where I am."

Greg tried working the ropes around his wrists, but they were too tight. Was it really worth prolonging the inevitable? There couldn't possibly be any satisfaction in knowing why Gabriella wanted to watch him suffer. The problem was, he couldn't help himself.

"I always thought you were some rich girl who was obsessed with the hood. Probably the head cheerleader at some private school in Orange County."

"Shit. I never even made it to high school thanks to my drunk-ass dad. Got mixed up with some gangbangers downtown when I was in eighth grade and the next thing you know I was in the life."

Greg tried to imagine her as a skinny little kid, scared but acting tough. He wondered how she managed to survive without a single tattoo or scar on her perfect body. He figured she would tell him eventually, if he just kept her talking.

"I was Big J's girl. He used to call me *mariposa*—butterfly— because I could dress up all slutty and put on a show. I was like a distraction. They'd send me into clubs or house parties to check shit out, shake my ass, and report back. Then my crew would roll up and take care of business. We must have done that a thousand times."

He could hear the nostalgia in her voice, the little girl still proud of herself for impressing her fill-in father figure.

"Until your music career took off?"

"None of that happened until after Big J got capped. Our crew kind of fell apart without him. Some of them joined other gangs, others got on the straight and narrow. I got the hell out of downtown, went to stay with some friends in Virgil Heights. That's actually how I found out about you, from my new boyfriend."

Greg's body went rigid. Things were starting to click, and it was even worse than he could have imagined. He tried to play it cool, pretending like his voice wasn't shaking.

"Anybody I know?"

"I think so. His name was Manny."

Greg watched as she stood up, tracking her silhouette as it floated across the mixing room for the door into the studio. He saw the hand come through first, but it wasn't Gabriella's. A skinny kid in baggy pants and a white T-shirt emerged instead. He'd been wearing a baker's hat the last time Greg saw him.

The kid took one look at Greg, shook his head, and grinned.

"You're one stupid motherfucker."

Greg had to agree, but couldn't afford to let it show.

"So much for getting your act together. I guess this means you won't be working at that café anymore."

"They don't have to know what goes down tonight. I'll wash your blood off my hands and pretend like nothing ever happened."

Greg felt a strange sense of relief knowing he wasn't going to die by hanging. Unless the kid planned to use him as a punching bag after he was already dead.

"You started dating your brother's girlfriend after he got killed? That's pretty cold."

That stopped him in his tracks, but the look on his face didn't change. He was close enough to kick the stool out from under Greg now.

"You still don't get it, do you, pig? Manny found God inside. Told me I had to forgive you for shooting me and move on with my life once we got out. He said it was the only way we would ever find peace, or some stupid shit like that."

"And you didn't agree with him…"

"Hell no! I don't believe in anything but getting even. It's all I've been thinking about since that day in the alley. He threatened to rat me out unless I promised to leave you alone."

"So, you had your brother killed?"

Greg was so focused on the kid that he almost forgot about Gabriella, until her voice came through the speakers again. She sounded a little more intense this time, as if she was getting high off of the violence building up in the room.

"Some of my boys took care of him. Manny was an embarrassment."

The kid stepped forward, foot against the leg of the stool.

"Time to say goodbye, pig."

Greg arched his back, waiting for the bottom to drop out. He closed his eyes tight and gritted his teeth in anticipation of the end. The moments dragged on, giving him time to say silent goodbyes to all of the people in his life; friends he'd turned his back on when he needed them the most. Kristen. His son.

Slowly, but surely, Greg's thoughts turned to his brother Tim. He wondered what went through his head in those final moments. Tried to make peace with the fact that he would never know for sure what happened to his brother at the record store. Greg almost wished he believed in heaven so he could see Tim again. But there was no God in the recording studio with them; only desperate people trying to make sense of the brutal world they inhabited.

Greg opened his eyes to have one last look around when the outside door flung open. Five uniformed BCPD officers stormed in, waving their weapons. The two bodyguards who had been quietly lurking in the background pulled out their guns and fired. Bullets flew around the room, ricocheting off of cymbals and shredding the fronts of amps. The kid turned to run, slowly knocking the stool over before he went.

Greg's body dropped a few inches before snapping back and starting to swing. The air to his lungs was instantly cut off, causing him to thrash around in a spastic, swirling dance. His feet kicked out at the empty air as the rope burned its way into the soft skin around his neck. Every passing second was more painful than the last, until Greg was left wishing it was over. His head felt like it was about to explode as the cacophony all around him sputtered and popped. Bursts of golden light glittered at the edges of his vision, alternating with the cascading waves of blackness that consumed him.

His body jerked involuntarily one last time before it went still.

Chapter 21

*T*im didn't look a second older than the day he died. Greg stood up from the sofa, hesitant at first. He couldn't believe this was actually happening. It had been twenty years since they'd seen each other. Greg went over to where his brother was peering out the garage window, placing a hand on his shoulder. Tim didn't respond at all, his eyes fixed on something in the backyard. Greg stood on his toes, catching a glimpse of the terrible scene outside. The garden had been replaced with a wooden gallows, where two bodies swung side-by-side in the ocean breeze. The corpses were dressed exactly the same—jeans, hoodies, and low-top sneakers—except one was a skinny twenty-something and the other was a middle-aged man. Tim reached up with an ice-cold hand to grab him...

Greg's arm jerked upward, the handcuff catching his wrist. It was fastened to the metal rail on the hospital bed where he lay. The monitors connected to his chest beeped wildly as he flailed and thrashed. A team of doctors and nurses rushed in, calling his name to calm him down. Greg tried to scream out for his brother, but the words got caught in his bone-dry throat. He was struggling to get up—bucking the bodies pinning him down—when a fresh dose of narcotics hit his bloodstream. The blackness that followed was an empty void where time did not exist.

ᔐ

GREG WOKE UP EARLY the next morning. His transition into the living world was much slower this time around, thanks to the residual effects of the morphine. He opened his eyes slowly over the course of several minutes; only half fighting the urge to slip back into nothingness. It wasn't until somebody squeezed his hand that he decided there might be something worth waking up for.

He eased his head to the left, expecting to see Kristen, but found Junior instead.

"I'm guessing this isn't heaven."

His voice was a wispy grumble. She snorted, sucking back a sigh of relief.

"That ship sailed a long time ago. Thirsty?"

"Depends on what you've got."

She brought a plastic cup up, feeding the end of a straw between his lips. He took several small sips of water, each one working its way across his tongue and down his parched throat. His neck muscles ached with each tiny swallow.

"How long was I up there swinging?"

The look on her face was both tender and scolding.

"A minute or less. They say there shouldn't be any permanent damage."

"Then why am I still here?"

"They wanted to monitor you, mostly because you were severely dehydrated. Which should come as no surprise considering..."

"I drank half the vodka in The Bay Cities?"

Junior forced a dry laugh, her disappointment filling the room. Greg went on.

"Don't worry, the last thing I want right now is another drink."

"You promise?"

Greg didn't respond, so Junior let it go.

"What the hell were you doing at the Flores Estate?"

"Looking for answers, I guess. Where are Kristen and Timmy?"

"Gone. They went up to Deer Springs to stay with her sister."

Greg's chest felt like it might cave in.

"For how long?"

She opened her mouth to answer when Marco wandered in. He gripped a bouquet of Mylar "Get Well" balloons in his fist. The pink and blue ribbons got looped and tied off near Greg's handcuffs.

"Welcome back, you drunk."

Greg motioned to the needle in his arm.

"I've moved on to the hard stuff now."

Junior got up to leave, stopping in the doorway.

"I need to pick Chris up from the rehearsal space. He'll be happy to hear you're alive."

Greg watched her leave. Marco stepped in front of him, ruining the view.

"I'm kind of pissed off at you, bro."

"Then why are you here?"

"Had some questions that couldn't wait."

"About?"

"Gabriella."

The mention of her name sent Greg hurtling back into the recording studio. Gabriella's voice was crystal clear in his memory, taunting him all over again as he teetered on the brink of death. Greg pictured the mixing room door opening and the kid in the blue hat kicking the chair out from under him. Relived the seasick feeling of swinging from a rope.

Greg strained to sit up, the words rushing from his mouth.

"What happened to her?"

"She got away in the gunfight, her and that kid from the bakery."

Greg's memories of that night were patchy at best, but that didn't seem possible.

"How? There were cops everywhere."

"The bodyguards' guns were blasting, bro. They had the cops pinned down for a few minutes, so the two of them must have snuck out through the back. Every cop in town is hunting for them."

Greg couldn't believe all of this happened while he dangled from the ceiling.

"Where are the bodyguards?"

"Both dead."

Greg laid back, willing his heart to stop racing.

"It was them. They killed all those people at our shows."

"No shit. That cop in Santa Barbara figured it out. He's the one that tipped the BCPD off. But they weren't expecting to find you there."

Greg watched his friend go pale. It looked like he might be sick.

"Listen, Marco. I was out of my mind. Nothing made sense. I went there to—"

Marco nodded.

"Save your breath, bro. I got the answer I needed. Maybe I'll come see you when you get home."

Marco backed out of the room. He'd been gone for a few minutes before it dawned on Greg that he was all alone.

ॐ

GREG SPENT THE REST of that night answering questions for Detective Bowers at the hospital. Like everybody else, he couldn't figure out what Greg would have been doing up at the Flores Estate. Even when Greg explained it to him—came clean about going there to sleep with Gabriella—Detective Bowers kept pressing, looking for clues that tied him to the murders. He must have been disappointed when the hospital discharged Greg before the BCPD could fabricate a reason to arrest him.

It was close to midnight by then, so Greg took a taxi home. The house was dark when he arrived, and everything was silent. He climbed straight into bed, tossing and turning as he relived memories from the pool house studio. It didn't help that this was the first time he'd slept in the bedroom without Kristen since she left.

It was close to dawn when he finally gave up on sleep, getting up to make coffee instead. The house seemed unnaturally empty and still without the baby crying or his wife wandering around looking for a pacifier or a bottle. He pulled a chair out at the kitchen table and sat down to wait—for what, he wasn't quite sure. Greg worried he might sit there forever, drowning in the same terrible thoughts until there was no line between the present and past. The distinction was already iffy.

He sat there in silence trying to figure out when it had all gone wrong. Was it really Tommy's book that set it all in motion, or something long before that? Could it have been the moment he unwittingly stumbled into Grizzly Flats, or the night at the tidal pools when he rescued Junior and Chris from a serial killer? When his best friend got shot on stage at Eddie's, or when he shot that kid in the alley in Virgil Heights?

Greg reached up to scratch the rope burn around his neck, certain the answer was in front of him all along. Everything changed the day he found out his brother died. He still felt gutted remembering how the news ripped the heart from his chest, leaving him hollow and empty forever after. Every day since then had been about filling the void—whether drinking himself blind, having meaningless sex, surfing, becoming a cop, or playing the hero. His life had become an endless pursuit of external gratification, no matter the cost to him or his family and friends.

And it had finally caught up with him. Everything he'd fought so hard to avoid was right in front of his face now, demanding to be reckoned with. Greg still wasn't ready to confront it all, but no longer had a choice. He was wrestling with that uncomfortable reality when he remembered the question Officer Bob asked him. *Did you ever realize I'm not the one you needed to forgive?*

The coffeemaker sputtered and popped, exhaling a puff of fragrant steam. The noise pulled Greg out of his own head. He jumped up to pour himself a cup of coffee, taking it out onto the back deck. The sun was coming up in the east, filling the backyard with a pale-yellow light. Greg sipped at his mug while working out Officer Bob's riddle. The more he thought about it, the angrier he got.

Greg stood up, dropping his mug to the ground. He paced back and forth across the deck, his chest getting tighter as his mind whirled. The same sick need for escape was back again; only this time he had nowhere to go. His only hope for a little relief was out in the garage where he left it the other night; full bottles mixed in with the empties.

Greg cut across the backyard, lunging for the garage door. He was almost inside when he heard somebody open the back gate. Marco was standing there when he turned around, Tommy right behind him.

"I wanted to visit you at the hospital, but they said you got out last night."

Greg stepped back outside, closing the door behind him. He studied Tommy, making note of his stylish new wardrobe. It was clear somebody else was shopping for him these days.

"You guys want to come in? I've got coffee inside."

They followed him into the house, spreading out on the living room couch while he got their drinks. Greg's hands were shaking when he handed them their mugs. Marco noticed right away, but Tommy seemed oblivious.

"You can't keep yourself out of trouble, can you?"

Greg sat down in the armchair across from them.

"Never could. When did you get back to town?"

"Came in yesterday for a late-night talk show. That's where I was when I heard what happened. You doing alright?"

Greg gave Marco a sideways glance.

"Depends on who you ask."

Tommy set his mug down on the coffee table, rubbing his palms back and forth on his distressed jeans.

"Listen, man. I wanted to apologize."

"For what?"

"For ruining your life. I had no idea my book would turn your world upside down. That was never the goal."

"Don't sweat it. My life was a mess way before I met you."

They all laughed at once, cutting the tension in half. Tommy leaned back, talking to the ceiling.

"I heard Kristen left. With your son."

"It's nothing permanent. We'll work it out."

"I really hope so. It's one thing for you to almost get yourself killed—that's some everyday shit for you—but I'm not sure I could handle the guilt of tearing your family apart."

"Jesus, Tommy. Did you come here to bum me out? Let me make you guys some breakfast."

Greg went into the kitchen, flinging the refrigerator open. Anything was better than sitting around apologizing to each other. He piled eggs, bacon, and a stick of butter onto the counter, pulling down a box of pancake mix from the cupboard. His hand was on the burner knob when somebody got a call.

Marco reached into his pocket, pulling a phone up to his ear.

"What the hell are you doing up? I thought you worked the late shift last night."

Greg and Tommy both watched as Marco's jaw dropped.

"We're on our way."

He brought the phone down, shouting to Greg and Tommy as he headed for the backyard.

"Gabriella and her little friend are outside of my condo trying to get in. JJ's stuck inside."

Greg dropped what he was doing, racing to join Marco without any thought. His only plan was to grab the gun from the garage before climbing into Marco's car. He wasn't surprised when Tommy hesitated, lingering on the couch.

"Where the hell are you guys going?"

Greg slowed down on his way outside, trying to hide his disappointment. Tommy had been his partner for everything that happened at Grizzly Flats, but now he felt like a stranger.

"Don't worry about it, Tommy. It isn't your fight this time around."

"Why don't we call the cops?"

Greg was already halfway to the garage, screaming his response as he ran.

"Call them if you want. It never does much good."

He ran inside, groping for his gun in the dark space. Everything was just as he left it, the wreckage of the past few days strewn across the floor. The sound of Marco's revving engine rushed through the open door. Greg grabbed a mostly empty bottle of vodka, holding it up to the scant light. One drink might keep his hand from shaking if things got out of control, making his aim a little truer. But he knew there wasn't such a thing as one drink any more.

Greg was salivating as he tilted the bottle up to his lips. The first belt was barely down his throat when Marco bounded in. He charged across the room, swiping the bottle from out of Greg's grip.

"If you go, I go."

Marco jammed the lip of the bottle into his own mouth, draining it dry. He dropped it to the carpet with a hollow thud.

"Let's go."

§

IT WAS STILL EARLY, so the morning traffic was light. They sped along Bay Cities Boulevard in silence. Greg felt strange in the passenger seat, but the El Camino was still parked outside of the Flores Estate. He watched the old neighborhood flickering by out the window, hoping they would make it in time to save JJ. Greg wasn't sure he could live with another death on his conscience.

There were no police cars in sight when they pulled up outside of the building. It wouldn't be long before they arrived, but there was no time to waste. They both jumped out, scanning the landscape for any sign of Gabriella or the kid in the blue hat. Marco went over to the security gate, punching in the code to let them inside. The elevator was open in the silent lobby, but they took the stairs up to the third floor. Greg was in the lead, gun raised and back against the stairwell wall.

"Maybe I should go up there alone. You make sure they don't sneak up on us from behind."

"No way, bro. We're doing this together."

They made slow progress, inching their way up one stair at a time. The fire door was closed when they reached the landing. Greg motioned for Marco to stay still while he listened for any signs of a struggle. The silence that met their ears gave no indication of what awaited them inside.

Greg took up a position a few steps down while Marco eased the door open. The hallway outside of the condo was empty, but the front door was open a crack. They were skulking along the wall when JJ started shrieking in terror. Whatever they were doing to him in there, it didn't sound like he would survive very long.

There was no time for a plan. Greg exchanged a knowing look with Marco before kicking the door open to tumble inside. He came up with his sights trained on the living room, eyes scanning furniture in the otherwise empty space. Marco bounded in behind him, quickly making his way into the kitchen. He grabbed a carving knife from the butcher's block before coming back to join Greg near the entrance.

"They must be in one of the bedrooms."

"Which one?"

Marco stepped over to where the closed bedroom doors stood side-by-side. He put his ear to JJ's, but didn't hear any movement or sound. He was about to do the same with his own door when a gunshot splintered the jamb from inside. There was a flurry of motion as Marco dove to the floor, chunks of wood and screams filling the air for a chaotic moment.

Greg took up a position behind the kitchen counter, his barrel trained on Marco's room.

"You guys are cornered! Let JJ go and come out with your hands up."

There was a hushed conversation in the bedroom followed by a tense silence. Greg couldn't understand what they said, but he knew something bad was about to happen. This wasn't some home invasion robbery gone wrong. The only reason they'd come there was to lure Greg and Marco back, and now it was time to finish what they started.

Marco sensed it, too. He slowly got up, backing around the corner and out of sight in the living room. The seconds dragged by, Greg's trigger finger tightening with every little sound. He was so on edge that he almost fired when the bedroom door finally swung open. The woman who emerged was a stranger. Her fashionable clothes were replaced with baggy pants and a flannel shirt. She sauntered forward, teasing him with her glare.

"What's the matter? Don't recognize me?"

Greg looked past her into the bedroom. He saw his bass player in there, bound to a chair with blood running from both nostrils. The kid in the blue hat stood behind him, the barrel of a gun pressed against JJ's temple.

Greg's eyes flicked back to Gabriella.

"You shouldn't have come back."

"I do what I want."

"And you wanted to get your throat cut?"

Marco lunged, grabbing her by the hair and pressing the knife against her neck. She tried to fight back, but he dug the blade deeper. A small line of blood was forming when Greg came out from behind the counter, brushing past her and into Marco's bedroom.

Greg tried to ignore the pleading look JJ gave him. He focused on the kid in the blue hat instead.

"Drop your gun and you might leave here alive."

The kid's voice was flat and emotionless, betraying fear on his face.

"My life's over either way. I die here or in prison."

Greg didn't have a good answer, not so soon after almost checking out himself. His life flashed before him as he swung from the rope that night, and he wasn't proud of what he saw. Even the good memories were stained by the violence, betrayal, and anger swirling around him like his own personal thunderstorm. There simply wasn't enough time to make all the apologies he owed, especially not when he made new mistakes every day.

"That's up to you. The only thing I care about right now is my friend. Put the gun down and let him go."

"Screw you, pig!"

The kid lifted his gun from JJ's head, but didn't get far. Greg fired three rounds without hesitation. Two of them caught the kid in the chest, the third shattering the window behind him. The sounds of the outside world rushed in, mixing with JJ's whimpers. The kid stumbled backward, collapsing to the floor. His head came to rest at an odd angle against the baseboard, the blue hat on the carpet at his side. Greg didn't have to check his pulse to know he was dead.

October 1998—8:00 p.m.

Tim was behind the counter when two young girls shuffled over. Both sported ratty, bleached-blonde hair dyed pink at the tips. He couldn't tell if their Catholic-schoolgirl uniforms were a fashion statement, or if they'd been wandering the streets since classes let out earlier that afternoon. They watched him clean scratches from used CDs until he looked up.

"Can I help you with something?"

The girl on the right produced a 7-inch from behind her back. Tim recognized the cover immediately, since he was the designer. It featured a photocopied picture of him and his brother skateboarding in an empty pool near their dad's house. They'd taken it shortly before the band formed, back in junior high. The four tracks on that single were the first songs Bad Citizen Corporation ever recorded. Only two hundred and fifty of them were ever pressed. Tim didn't even own one himself any more.

She set it on the counter, along with a Sharpie.

"Can we have your autograph?"

Tim picked it up carefully, as though it were made of glass. He was disappointed they weren't there to sell the rare artifact. Not that he had the money to buy it.

"Where'd do you guys find this?"

"At a garage sale, down by the beach. We've listened to it like a thousand times."

He flipped it over, reading the hand-written liner notes. The studio where they recorded those songs was a restaurant now. His guitar from that session had long ago been hocked for dope.

The girl on the right blew a bubble, covering her lips when it popped. Tim grabbed the marker, removing the cap with his teeth before getting to work. His signature was an unrecognizable squiggle, so small it was hard to see.

The two girls squealed as they ran from the store. Tim waited until they were gone before he let himself smile. It was erased a few seconds later when a familiar face came through the front door. Tim watched with dread as BCC's sleazy new manager, Mikey Fitzgerald, approached. He slammed his briefcase down on the counter, snapping the locks open with his thumbs.

"I'm glad you're here, Tim."

"Where else would I be?"

"I don't know…passed out in a gutter somewhere? But that's none of my business anymore. Or at least it won't be once you sign these documents."

Tim guessed Mikey was the only twenty-something wearing a sport coat within ten miles of his record store. The new wardrobe didn't change Tim's opinion that he was nothing more than a weasel with slicked back hair and bright white teeth. He hated everything Mikey tried to be; and everything he forced BCC to become.

"I already told you, I'm not signing shit. You want to play Malcolm McLaren? Leave me out of it."

Mikey pulled out a folder, flipping it open to reveal a stapled contract. He spun it around on the counter to face Tim, setting a ballpoint pen on top of it.

"Like it or not, Bad Citizen Corporation is a business partnership. We have to finalize your departure before your brother can move on with his career."

Tim pushed the documents back at Mikey, sending the pen and folder to the floor.

"There weren't any contracts when I started the band, so we don't need one now."

Mikey bent down to pick them up, straightening his sleeves when he stood again. He set the folder and pen back on the counter, a flush of red building up on his cheeks. Tim couldn't decide what was more fun—signing an autograph for those two girls, or watching this asshole lose his cool. It was too early to tell, but Tim decided to celebrate with a speedball either way. He just had to get rid of this asshole first.

"If you don't mind, I've got work to do."

Mikey made a show of looking around the empty store.

"How rude of me. I should come back when you aren't so busy."

"Or don't come back at all."

Tim stepped out from behind the counter, heading for the office. He walked down a short hallway plastered with gig flyers featuring the names all of his favorite bands. Tim took a seat behind the desk. Mikey entered the room seconds after him.

"You're only putting off the inevitable. BCC is going on without you, whether you like it or not."

Tim leaned back, trying not to think about the syringe in the top drawer. He wouldn't give Mikey the satisfaction of watching him fix.

"Where's Greg?"

"Excuse me?"

"You know, my so-called brother. Why isn't he here if this is so important?"

Mikey put his hands down on the desk, shoulders sagging. It was as close to human as Tim had ever seen him.

"Listen. I don't want to get involved in any family matters, but it's hard not to make this situation personal. The truth is, your brother doesn't want to see you. He's the one who sent me down here to get these papers signed."

"That's bullshit and you know it!"

Mikey brought his hands up in a defensive posture.

"Whoa, whoa, whoa. Don't kill the messenger. You and Greg haven't spoken in—what—weeks? Whatever's going on between you two, it has nothing to do with me. This is strictly business as far as I'm concerned."

Tim jumped up, pacing the room. Everything Mikey said made sense, but he didn't want to believe it. The more he thought about it, the angrier he got. The angrier he got, the more he wanted to get rid of Mikey so he could get high.

"You guys can't have the name unless Greg comes down here to ask me himself."

"Come on, Tim. You know that isn't going to happen. Why stand in his way?"

"He wouldn't even be playing in a band if it weren't for me."

"Which is why he wants to keep the name alive. You've already said you're done with music, so it's worthless to you. Unless..."

Tim stepped right up to Mikey, until the tips of their noses were practically touching. It felt unnatural for him to be so aggressive. That was always more Greg's style.

"Unless what?"

"Maybe there's a part of you that doesn't want Greg to succeed. It would make sense for you to be jealous."

"Jealous my ass. I just want to hear it from him."

In the end, it was Mikey who backed down. He wandered over to the office door, leaning against the jamb.

"I'll tell him, but it won't make a difference. My guess is he'd rather start a whole new band than have to deal with any of this."

"What the hell's that supposed to mean?"

"Look around. You're killing yourself, but all you can think about is ruining Greg's future before you check out. Why don't you do him a favor—do us all a huge fucking favor—and get it over with. Maybe then you're brother can have the music career he deserves, without any interference from you."

Tim slumped down into his chair again, completely exhausted and dope sick. He just wanted to be alone so he could shoot up. Nothing else mattered any more.

"Maybe you're right."

"I'm sorry?"

"Bring me the papers. I'll sign them."

Chapter 22

Greg paddled with both arms, letting the momentum of the wave catch his board. He pushed himself up in a practiced motion, maintaining his balance as the Pacific slid away beneath him. The folding wall of water chased him down the line, but he managed to stay ahead of it; carving and cutting his way across a momentary ripple on the ocean. And when his perfect ride was over, he tumbled and spun in the aftermath until the water finally freed him.

He emerged in the whitewash, gasping for air. It wasn't getting harder to hold his breath, but Greg was more aware of his breathing these days. The wetsuit chafed at the rope burns around his neck as the leash pulled him a few feet closer to shore. Marco and Chris were still behind him, looking to catch perfect rides of their own. Greg stood up, tucked the board under one arm, and plodded his way to dry sand.

Junior held up a towel when he arrived. Greg unzipped his wetsuit, shimmying out of his rubbery skin.

"My dad was here a second ago."

Greg set his eyes on the horizon, where a group of paddle boarders formed a circle. Their silhouettes looked small and blurry in the distance.

"I'm glad the Sober SUP group's working out for him."

"You could go join them, you know."

He slipped a T-shirt on, wrapping the towel around the outside of his board shorts.

"I think I'm done for today."

"They'll be there tomorrow, too."

"Thanks for the surf report, Junior."

He sat down beside her, watching the sets roll in. Afternoon sunlight sparkled on the water, reflecting blue skies overhead. Junior elbowed him, nodding to a sunbathing woman a few yards away. She was laying on her stomach and reading *Among the Grizzlies*.

Junior shaded her eyes, laughing out loud.

"You're never going to escape that book."

"No shit. I just hope Tommy doesn't write another one after everything that happened this month."

"At least he wasn't around to take notes this time."

"Something tells me that won't stop him."

She reached out, putting a hand on his.

"Do you still think BCC will record an album, now that the murders have been solved? Chris wanted to ask, but didn't know how."

"Probably not any time soon."

Chris and Marco charged up, dropping their boards on the sand to get changed. Greg noticed Chris was almost a foot taller than Marco now. He wondered if his own son would sprout up in his teens, and if he'd be around to see it. Or if Timmy would end up dead, like the kid in the blue hat. Those were the dark possibilities dancing around his head now that things had finally calmed down. That didn't mean he was ready to deal with any of it.

Greg stood, slapping Marco on the shoulder.

"You ready to head back up to the house? I still need to clean up the office before we start looking for more work."

Marco smiled, shaking the sand from his wet hair.

"You're a slave driver, bro."

They said goodbye to Junior and Chris, making plans to barbecue on Sunday afternoon. The sand was hot, but their soles were thick and calloused from a lifetime spent on the beach. Neither of them said much until they reached the house.

Greg leaned his board against the garage and disappeared inside. He emerged moments later with a full bottle of vodka in his hand. Marco went into the kitchen, grabbing two glasses of ice and a carton of orange juice. They met at the table on the back deck, mixing up cocktails in silence.

They never talked about their drinking. It was just a fact again, like the scars and tattoos covering their bodies. They could try to hide it, but sooner or later somebody would notice. Greg decided he'd done enough hiding.

Marco lifted his glass in a toast.

"To running away from our problems."

Greg could drink to that.

"You write that one?"

"Hell no. An old-school surfer said it in some interview I read."

Greg could drink to that, too. And when his glass was empty, he mixed himself another one. This was the first time in a long time he didn't have anywhere to be—unless he counted looking for his wife and son. He took a swig, deciding to give it a few more days. Kristen and Timmy were safe where they were, and Greg wasn't feeling much like a husband or father. *They'll either come home on their own, or we'll all agree it's better for them to stay away for good.*

Marco snatched the bottle, pouring himself another. He added so little orange juice that his cocktail was the color of piss.

"Been thinking about your brother a lot lately."

"Kind of hard not to with everything that happened."

"You ever miss him?"

It was a good question. Greg had been angry with Tim for years, but it usually sprang up when he least expected it. These days, between Tommy's book and the murders, Tim was on his mind all the time. It felt like he'd been resurrected in the worst possible way—twenty years too late and without any new information about the night he died.

Greg felt his blood beginning to boil. His beverage put out the fire.

"What do you think happened that night at the record store?"

Marco shuddered, a pained expression hijacking his face. He tried to speak several times, but the words wouldn't form.

"Jesus, Marco. If you've got one of your crazy theories cooking, spit it out."

"I was there."

Greg sat up, scooting to the edge of his chair. It felt like the glass might shatter in his tightening grip.

"*You were there?*"

"I needed a place to shoot up. Tim let me use his office sometimes when the record store was open. And…"

"What?!"

"And I broke in sometimes at night to steal CDs. My dealer used to take them in trade."

"Stealing from your friends. Typical junkie crap. What happened with Tim?"

"I don't know. He was alive when I left the first time."

Greg stood, his heart was pounding. He tried to control his voice, to keep Marco talking, but it got harder with each new piece of information. It took everything in him not to leap across the table and throttle his partner.

"*The first time?* What the hell did you two talk about?"

"The band, mostly. He said something about Mikey making him sign over the name to you. Then he gave me twenty bucks and I split. That's all I remember, bro."

"What about when you came back?"

Marco gripped the arms of his chair. His face was pale and beads of sweat formed on his forehead. Greg thought he might be on the verge of a heart attack.

"It was the middle of the night. I tried to get him down, but he'd already checked out. I took a few CDs and the money from the cash box, and bailed."

The missing money was something Greg always held onto. Proof that his brother was killed during a robbery. And now he knew the truth. It was like an old splinter was removed after years of discomfort, replaced by a knife in his back.

"So, you robbed your dead friend? Did you even bother to call the police?"

"Yes…but not until later."

"After you scored."

"It's not a big secret I was an addict. That's why I called in an anonymous tip."

Greg turned this new information over in his head, inspecting it for flaws. He'd wanted answers for years, but not like this. Not when the new facts proved Officer Bob was right all along. He jumped up, grabbing Marco by the shirt.

"Why didn't you tell me?!"

"I don't know. I didn't think it mattered. He was already...gone."

Greg shoved Marco backward into the chair, digging knuckles into his chest.

"What else do you know?"

"Nothing, bro. It was a long time ago."

Greg saw genuine fear in his friend's eyes. He released him, backing away. It was either that or snap his neck.

"You need to leave. Right now."

Greg grabbed the bottle, heading for the garage. He was half way across the yard when a car pulled up behind the back fence. The lights mounted on the roof were a bad sign; things were about to get worse. Greg looked over his shoulder to make sure Marco had seen it too.

They were both standing when Detective Bowers came through the gate. He was alone, but moved like he was raiding the place. The only thing missing was a drawn gun.

He sneered at the bottle in Greg's hand.

"You two having a little celebration?"

"More like a wake. What the fuck do you want?"

Detective Bowers kept walking until they were face-to-face.

"Who are you mourning, exactly? The kid you shot or all the kids that died because of you?"

"We went over this at the station the other night. He pointed his gun at me. JJ backed me up on that, and Gabriella copped to the murders. Case closed."

Bowers brought a hand up, poking a finger into Greg's chest.

"I'm still not convinced."

Greg took a step back, brushing his hand away. He saw a fire ignite inside of Detective Bowers when their skin made contact. Marco came up behind Greg, forcing himself between them.

"Step away, bro. He's trying to wind you up."

Detective Bowers took one look at Marco and laughed.

"I'm glad you're here too. I had an interesting chat with Gabriella today. She said she stayed with you during the tour. That true?"

Marco gave Greg a sideways glance. His jaw was tight and his brow was furrowed. It wasn't easy to tell if this new information was sinking in. Marco guessed he had about thirty seconds before everything went sideways.

"Maybe we should do this down at the station. You know, like, when we're sober."

Detective Bowers brushed Marco off.

"Answer the question. Does your partner here know you were sneaking a murderer into your hotel rooms at night?"

Marco spun to leave.

"Fuck this. I'm out of here."

Detective Bowers' hand shot out, yanking him to the ground by his collar. Marco threw elbows, trying to fight back. That only made Detective Bowers angrier. He slid his forearm around Marco's neck, pulling it tight.

Greg didn't blink, bringing the bottle across the officer's head. It made a hollow sound when it connected with his skull. The glass didn't shatter, but Detective Bowers crumpled.

Greg was on him before he hit the ground. He followed up with a kick to the gut before delivering a barrage of punches to the face. Detective Bowers curled up into a fetal position, trying in vain to cover his head with both arms. Greg unloaded blow after blow, spitting and grunting as he unleashed every ounce of energy in his body. He saw the nose snap first, felt a sense of satisfaction at the blood bursting up into the air. Next came the jaw, twisting to the left from the force of Greg's fist.

Detective Bowers lie motionless beneath him, but Greg didn't relent. He yanked his limp body up by the shirt, slamming him down to the ground again and again. Greg watched the vacant eyes roll back in his head, blood smeared across his destroyed face. Something in the back of Greg's head told him to stop—that the fight was over—but he didn't know how. He might have killed him if it weren't for his partner.

Marco dove at Greg, knocking him to the ground beside Detective Bowers. Greg's first instinct was to keep fighting, but his muscles wouldn't comply. His chest heaved and his head throbbed as utter exhaustion settled in. He lay there motionless listening to Detective Bowers gurgling and wheezing, fighting for every gasp of air. Marco muttered *'Fuck. Fuck. Fuck.'* under his breath, pulling out his phone to dial 911.

Greg was spent. He closed his eyes, waiting for whatever was going to come next.

Chapter 23

Greg didn't dream that night because he never really slept. His nightmares found him with his eyes wide open. There was nobody else in the holding cell to disturb him, but the voices in his head were screaming. He looked down at the battered knuckles on his right fist, swallowed up by swollen, puffy skin. That hand had done more damage over the years than any gun he ever held. And now it might be a murder weapon, too.

He carefully stretched his fingers out, feeling the tiny broken bones inside as they scraped against each other. There was something soothing about the pain pulsing through his wrist and arm. A persistent reminder of the pain he'd inflicted, as if he could ever forget.

He stood up again, walking a familiar circle around the cold concrete floor. The bars, benches, and toilet passed by in a blur, like they had in the countless laps he'd already made. Unwanted images of Detective Bowers' bludgeoned face cycled through his head with every step he took. He studied each one, burning them into the backs of his eyelids. This wasn't some lingering nightmare he could escape from, but the inevitable future he'd always managed to kick down the road.

The only thing he had to look forward to now was sentencing, followed by a violent death at the hands of a fellow inmate. He'd seen first-hand what could happen to ex-cops in prison and it wasn't pretty. Unless a few of Detective Bowers' squad got to him first. Greg knew some of them thirsted for revenge, if they only got the chance. Either way, it was looking like his last hour on earth would be brutal.

Greg stopped to look up. There was nothing in the ceiling that could hold his weight, but the crossbars over the door might do the trick. He wondered how many desperate people had taken their lives there, or at least had the same idea. His hand wandered down to the empty belt loops on his jeans. The arresting officer had taken his shoelaces too. Everything else in the cell was furniture, and all of it was bolted down. The BCPD had covered all their bases. *Looks like I'm not getting out of this that easy.*

He laid down on the narrow aluminum bench, willing himself to sleep. This was always the final action in the sequence he'd been repeating for the last six hours—stare at his hands, think about what he'd done, pace the cell, and try to fall asleep. The crook of his elbow was over his eyes when he heard a door creaking open. He sat up to see if he was getting a cellmate, or if it was time for his beat down.

He was surprised when Officer Bob came through the door instead. It looked like he'd aged ten years since Greg last saw him. His head was shaved clean, shoulders sagging. It took him a while to make his way down the hall. Greg was ready for him when he arrived.

"Visiting hours?"

Officer Bob pulled a folding chair over, sitting a few feet outside of Greg's reach. The bars between them became more solid for Greg now, a reminder of how different the two of them had always been.

"They treating you all right?"

"The arresting officer got a little rough putting me in the cruiser, but who could blame him? The interrogation was by the book."

Officer Bob nodded, folding his legs. His voice was hoarse.

"I might have forced a fight and shot you, if it was me."

"You had plenty of opportunities to do that over the years. Don't try to act tough now."

"Maybe you're right. You have a lawyer?"

"Public defender. Lucky me."

Greg wondered if the smile on his face looked as fake as it felt. Officer Bob had bigger questions on his mind.

"Why'd you do it, Greg? Why'd you finally snap?"

Greg stood up to pace again, a few minutes ahead of schedule. It never occurred to him to consider the reasons for what he'd done. As far as he was concerned, Detective Bowers pushed the wrong guy too far. Looking back, it seemed like one of them was destined to end up in the hospital since the moment they met.

Officer Bob demanded an answer.

"He has a family, you know? A wife and two little girls."

The meaningless words reflected off the cinderblock walls. Greg didn't have the headspace to worry about anybody else's family at the moment.

"Maybe he should have been at home with them instead of at my place, harassing me and trying to choke Marco out."

"He was doing his job. If anybody can understand that, it should be you."

"He was an aggressive asshole with a chip on his shoulder."

"Does that justify what you did to him? He's in a coma, for Christ's sake. Fighting for his life."

That almost knocked the wind out of Greg. Nobody had given him an update on Detective Bowers since the ambulance pulled away the previous night. He took a seat, trying to process this new information. His face was still in his hands when Officer Bob went on.

"I spent my whole career trying to avoid this moment. Ever since you were a little kid, I felt this need to protect you from yourself." He folded his arms, gaze dropping to his shoes. "I guess I let us both down."

"This has nothing to do with you. You weren't even there."

"It's not about what happened last night, but all the years leading up to it. There were a thousand times I could have thrown you in jail, but I always found a way to let it slide. Any one of those opportunities might have changed this outcome."

Greg exhaled loudly, fighting back tears.

"I don't think so, Bob. It might not have been Detective Bowers, but I'm starting to think it was always going to end this way."

Officer Bob stood up, angling for the exit.

"Maybe you're right, Greg. I still wish we could have stopped it."

Greg clutched the bars, pressing his head against them to watch him leave.

"What's going to happen now?"

Officer Bob stopped at the end of the hall, the door already open. He stared at Greg, a look of pained concentration on his face.

"Did you ever figure out who you should forgive for your brother's death?"

Greg made a show of considering the question, but he already knew the answer. It had been there all along, right in front of his face. Tim really did kill himself. He was a desperate junkie who came to the conclusion life was no longer worth living. But he only got there—took his final step into nothingness—because Greg turned his back on him. *It's no wonder I was so willing to let my family go. I've been doing it my whole life.*

"Sorry, Officer Bob. Forgiveness has to be earned."

"In that case, Mr. Salem, I hope you earn some soon. You're really going to need it where you're going."

Officer Bob stepped out of view, the door closing behind him. Greg lingered for a moment, hoping somebody else would come to see him. He sat on the bench eventually, leaning back to lay down. New thoughts swirled around his head as he stared up at the ceiling. Greg wondered if he ever truly would forgive himself, or if he'd spend the rest of his life picking fights and playing the hero. There was no time for reprieve, remorse, or reflection as long as he kept moving.

Greg got up, started pacing again. Life was too short to sit still.

—THE END—

Acknowledgments

Greg Salem was conjured on a midnight drive through the heart of California. I molded my punk-rock PI and his colorful crew over the next couple of years, using them to populate a fictional universe set against the backdrop of SoCal's legendary hardcore scene. While shaping the original story about a disgraced cop in the midst of a midlife crisis, I discovered I had three books in mind. You're holding the third one now, and that still blows my mind. Whether this is your introduction to the series, or you've read the trilogy, thank you for exploring the dark corners of the sunny beach towns where I grew up.

So many friends, fellow authors, and musical idols have indirectly supported, influenced, or inspired my writing that it would be impossible to acknowledge all of them. For now I'll stick to the smaller circle that helped bring *Hang Time* into the world. First and foremost, thanks to my wife, Heather, and our kids for giving me the room to write. To my beta readers, Paul Covington and Scott Ross, for their brutal honesty and often hilarious insights. A shout out to my editor, Elaine Ash, for sticking with this series since the beginning. Thanks to David Ivester at Author Guide for getting the word out about Greg Salem. And to my lawyer, Kim Thigpen, and my agent, Amy Moore-Benson, for their steady guidance and advice.

Last, but certainly not least, I'd like to thank Tyson Cornell, Alice Elmer, Hailie Johnson, Julia Callahan, and the team at Rare Bird Books for publishing *Bad Citizen Corporation*, *Grizzly Season* and *Hang Time*.

For more information about S. W. Lauden or the Greg Salem trilogy, visit www.swlauden.com.